Chapter 1

One ordinary day, just outside the city of Akomant, Phinn swims around Turtle Lake in search of his brother Ginn who supposedly lives there. Phinn's brother Dinn sits on the shore watching him.

A fisherman stands on a dock a few feet away from Dinn. When the fisherman lifts the fish he just caught out of the water, Phinn leaps out of the lake as well and snatches it right out from under him.

"Hey!" The man shouts as he throws an empty beer can at the location where Phinn reentered the water. The dolphin pops his head out of the lake to scold him.

"Excuse me; that's called littering. Get in here and get your trash out of the water right now!"

"Hell no. You took my catch."

The fisherman throws another beer can into the lake, this time hitting Phinn in the face.

"Oh, now you've done it." Phinn warns as his anger mounts.

"Done what? This?"

The man hits Phinn with yet another beer can, however, this time, the can was still full.

That last attack was the tipping point for Phinn as he jumps out of the lake and onto the dock, then quickly grabs the fisherman and hurls him into the water next to his beer cans.

"Did you think that was a request? It wasn't. It was a demand. Now I'll tell you again. Get your garbage out of the lake and then say you're sorry."

The man tries to swim back to shore without collecting his trash but Phinn prevents him from doing so by wandering back and forth in front of each place he tries to reach land from.

"Hey, idiot, get out of the way!" The fisherman calls out.

"That's an awfully funny way to say I'm sorry."

"You're the one who should be sorry. What do you think is going to pollute the lake more: a couple of aluminum cans or my dead body?"

Phinn lets out a confused squeak.

"Yeah, that's right. I'll die if you leave me in here forever."

"I don't want to leave you in there forever." Phinn responds. "Just long enough for you to figure how to pick up your garbage. Or are you mentally incapable of such a thing?"

The fisherman grunts and then starts swimming as fast as he can in the other direction. Phinn takes the man's fishing rod and casts it out towards him, catching him on the shirt with the hook. He then starts to reel the man in.

"I got a big one!"

The fisherman continues to try and swim away but the much larger dolphin is able to easily overpower him. Phinn shows off his prize to his brother.

"Look what I got! I'd say this is about a two-hundred pounder. Hurry Dinn; take a picture."

"I don't have a camera."

"Then take a mental picture."

"No. I don't want to."

"Fine. But now thanks to you no one is going to believe that a caught a human this big."

Phinn unhooks the fisherman who then runs off while leaving all of his stuff behind. The dolphin laughs as walks over to sit down next to his brother.

"Did you find Ginn?" Dinn asks.

"No. I searched the lake from top to bottom and from shore to shore but I couldn't find him anywhere. Are you sure this is the right lake?"

Dinn nods. "I'm sure. And I'm not surprised that you couldn't find him. I told you that he lives **on** a lake, not **in** a lake. He actually lives in that house right over there."

Dinn points to a fancy two story house on the other side of the lake. Phinn looks over at it and then back at his brother.

"So you let me waste all that time for nothing?"

"Yep." Dinn answers with a laugh.

Phinn starts laughing as well.

"That's what I would've done to you too."

The two dolphins laugh together for a second before Phinn gets serious.

"Alright let's go over there already."

Phinn and Dinn swim across the lake over to Ginn's house with Phinn collecting the three beer cans along the way. Once they arrive, Dinn knocks on the front door. Ginn answers it a few seconds later.

"What is this trash doing on my doorstep?" He asks sounding totally appalled.

Phinn squeaks in shock. "Well excuse me. Is that the way you talk about your younger brothers? I thought our parents would have raised you better than that. I'm assuming they would have if that hadn't abandoned us as kids that is."

"Just calm down Phinn; I was talking about the beer cans you're holding." Ginn convincingly lies.

"Oh right. Some jerk threw these in the lake. You got some place where I can recycle them?"

"Nah."

"Alright then."

Phinn drops the beer cans on Ginn's doorstep and then barges his way through the front door with Dinn following right behind him.

"So Dinn tells me that you have a nice place. And by the looks of it, he isn't lying. So the question remains: why haven't you invited me to stay with you before now?"

"Ahh…"

Phinn gives Ginn a playful slap across the face, though it still leaves a mark.

"I'm just messing with you. I had a place of my own. Until some humans ruined it. Which is why I'm here actually. You want to help me beat them up?"

"Now's not a good time actually. And actually it's a good thing that you showed up here. My wife Lynn's about to give birth. You should probably be here to name it as soon as possible."

"Why does Phinn get to name your kid?" Dinn asks. "Why not me?"

"Because when we were kids Phinn had a ball that I really wanted so I traded him the rights to name my firstborn child for it."

"I was just going to throw that ball away once I got a new one so I figured I might as well get **something** for it." Phinn states.

"Does Lynn know about this?"

"I've mentioned it to her, yes. I promised her you weren't going to pick something stupid and she was…okay with it."

Phinn laughs. "Big mistake. You shouldn't make promises you know you can't keep."

"Well can I get the middle name at least?" Dinn questions. "I want it to be Dinn but only if the baby's cute. If you get an ugly baby, I don't want to have any part of that."

"We'll see. Dinn's a boy's name. We don't know if it's going to be a boy or a girl yet."

"Where is your wife anyway?" Phinn asks.

"Right here." Lynn says as she enters the room. "It's time."

The three brothers follow Lynn outside. She dives into the lake with Phinn following right behind her. Lynn stops swimming and comes to the surface when she realizes how close Phinn is behind her.

"Can I have a little space, please? I really don't need your help for this part."

"Sorry. No problem."

Lynn dives back underwater and continues her swim while, this time, Phinn follows her around but at a much larger distance away, speeding up only to grab the baby, a boy, right after she gives birth to him. Phinn returns to shore with the newborn.

"I'm going to name you Dorsal. That way, when we're together, we'll be Dorsal-Phinn." He says with a loud laugh.

Lynn jumps out of the water to confront her brother-in-law.

"Hey Phinn! You just screwed up. You were supposed to name him something that rhymes with Phinn, not something related to a body part."

Phinn shrugs. "Oh well. Not my baby."

He hands Dorsal over to his mother who is still clearly upset.

"And you Ginn. Why'd you tell him what was going on? We were so close to getting out of it. Why'd you have to invite him over here?"

"I didn't invite him. He just showed up. Besides, I made a deal. You can't expect me to go back on my word. We even had that deal notarized and everything."

Ginn shows his wife the legal document detailing his and Phinn's trade.

"I understand you not wanted to break the contract. I just wish Phinn would have stayed home and forgotten about it. That's all."

"Me too." Phinn announces. "But humans kicked me out of my home. Want to go beat them up with me?"

"I kind of would right about now but I've got to stay here with…Dorsal."

"He can come too. It'd be a great learning experience for him. I heard that children who are exposed to violence at an early age are ten times more likely to be normal when they grow up."

"No, Phinn. You're thinking of less likely."

"Possibly. You'd think it'd be one or the other. So you going to go with me or what?"

"I'll have to pass."

"What about Dorsal? You didn't ask him if **he** wanted to go. I could take him for you if you want?"

"Dorsal's going to pass too. I still can't believe you'd give such a cute baby such an awful name. What a shame. And what an idiot you are, Phinn."

"A cute baby you say?" Dinn interrupts. "I guess his middle name is Dinn now."

"That's a lot better than what Phinn came up with." Lynn replies. "If we left it up to him his middle name would probably be kidney or something."

Phinn squeaks in confusion. "Kidney Phinn? That doesn't make any sense. Just like it doesn't make any sense that Ginn created such a cute baby. He's the ugliest one of the four brothers. It goes me, then Dinn, then Zinn, and then Ginn."

Dinn nods. "I agree. Except you accidentally put you before for me when it should be the other way around."

"No. That was on purpose."

"I know. That was just my polite way of saying you made a mistake."

"Excues me." Ginn interjects. "You've both made a mistake. I'm the cutest brother. That's why it makes sense for me to have a cute baby."

Phinn shakes his head. "No. Ginn, you're the ugliest. That's an undisputable fact."

"No it isn't. We're all going to say we're the cutest so let's just agree to disagree."

"No. Let's agree to agree with me." Phinn replies.

"Why would we do that?" Ginn asks. "Let's ask an unbiased third party instead."

"That's sounds fair." Dinn acknowledges. "Who'd you have in mind?"

"My wife, Lynn. So Lynn, tell us. Which one of us is the cutest?"

Lynn shakes her head in frustration.

"No. I'm not answering that. I'm mad at all of you right now. To me you're all pretty ugly…on the inside. I'm taking Dorsal inside."

Lynn brushes past the brothers who stay together outside.

"Just on the inside? I can live with that." A relieved Phinn says.

"Thanks for getting me in trouble, Phinn." Ginn sarcastically declares.

Phinn gives his brother a comforting pat on the back.

"You know what would make you feel better?" He asks. "Beating up some humans. Let's go do it."

"I suppose." Ginn sighs.

Chapter 2

Ace sits with his friends in his school's auditorium, chewing gum and then throwing it at the people sitting in the seats below him as he waits for the presentation the entire fifth grade was called in for to begin.

"I hope this isn't another drug prevention presentation." Grant comments. "It makes it more difficult for me to unload my product on people when they know it's bad for them. Why haven't the cigarette companies bribed the school district into spreading false information yet?"

"Nobody cares about your problems, Grant." Ace snaps. "Have you ever considered that the reason why it's difficult for you to unload your product is because you're a terrible salesman?"

He shakes his head no then attempts to explain why he so wholeheartedly disagrees with his brother.

"Actually, for your information, the reviews on the Dealr app say I'm a five star drug dealer. Friendly, discrete, available. These are all good things people are saying about me."

Grant takes out his phone and shows the group his Dealr profile containing over fifty five star reviews as proof.

"That many people can't be wrong."

Ace just waves off the whole thing.

"They can if they're all stupid. It doesn't matter though. I'm tired of talking about you. Hey, Curtis; can I have some more gum?"

"I already gave you all of my gum."

"What about that piece you're chewing on right now?"

"Dude, get a hold of yourself. It's over."

Ace sticks his hand out and waits for Curtis to spit his gum into it.

"Are you serious right now?"

Instead, Curtis spits the gum himself into the back of the neck of a kid sitting a couple rows down. They don't even notice what's been done to them.

"There. I did it for you. Now there's **absolutely** no more gum."

Ace folds his arms and pouts.

"Yeah, like that's what I wanted to have happen." He says with a roll of his eyes.

Ace then immediately rips a piece of the cushion off the arm of his chair, chews on it, and then spits it at the same kid that Curtis spat at. Afterwards he flexes his jaws and swipes at his tongue to try and get the taste out of his mouth.

"Ugh, I'm never doing that again."

"You shouldn't have done that a first time." Parker comments.

"You know what…"

Ace is cut off as loud party music begins playing and man dressed in a suit and wearing a headset runs out onto the stage and starts jogging in a circle.

"**Who wants to get excited**?" He shouts out to the crowd.

Ace jumps up and down in his seat and raises his hand to answer amid a low amount of cheers from the rest of the crowd.

"Me! I do! I want to get excited! Woooooooooo!"

The man stops running and now stands at the front of the stage facing the audience.

"**I can't hear you**. I said: **who wants to get excited**?"

"**Dude are you deaf? I said I did already**!" Ace shouts as the rest of the audience raises their volume as well.

The presenter seems to ignore Ace entirely.

"That's better. My name is Samuel Lawson and you all better be ready to get excited because I have some very exciting information to share with you. You're all going to get free prizes!"

The crowd cheers the loudest yet after hearing those words.

"If you sell enough boxes of Lawson Farms turkey balls that is. You're school has agreed to take part in a fundraiser by selling my family's products. A portion of the money you make from your sales will go to something this school desperately needs."

"I hope he's talking about a new computer lab." Parker declares. "That fire over the summer destroyed most of our current one. Now we're stuck using outdated junk."

"I was hoping he was talking about replacing the lead pipes leading to the drinking fountains." Rash adds.

Lawson resumes talking after giving time for the crowd to discuss what he might have been referring to.

"I'll tell you what that something is at the end of the program. But right now, wouldn't you like to hear more about the prizes?"

The crowd shouts "yes" in unison.

"That's what I thought. I'll go over the different levels of prizes right now."

A screen rolls down behind Lawson as Principal Fields turns on the projector to display the first slide.

"First we have level A. If you sell ten boxes of Turkey Balls, you'll get a free box of Lawson Farms turkey balls all for yourself. Selling twenty boxes gets you to level B where you'll get a key chain with the Lawson Farms Turkey mascot on it as well as the free box."

Lawson motions for Fields to turn to the next slide.

"Next we have level D for some reason."

"Sorry, I think I double clicked it." Principal Fields informs. "Want me to turn back?"

"No, don't worry about. You can't go from better back to worse or else people will be disappointed."

"Alright then. You're the boss."

Lawson turns his attention back to the screen.

"Well, you've all gotten a good look at level D. It's one hundred boxes and you get a Lawson Farms foam football. Doesn't that look like fun? Alright next slide."

Principal Fields turns ahead just one slide this time. He breathes a small sigh of relief when he sees that he didn't make another mistake.

"And here we have levels E and F. If you sell two-hundred and fifty boxes then you get all the prizes from the previous levels, **plus** this t-shirt."

Lawson unfurls a shirt that has a turkey giving a thumbs-up with the phrase "yummy!" underneath it. He rolls it up into a ball and tries throwing it into the audience but it only lands near the feet of a kid in the front row. That kid immediately bends over to pick it up.

"That one's free but if you sell two-hundred and fifty boxes you'll still get another one just so you know that. And if you manage to sell a staggering **five-hundred** boxes you'll get this added to your prize pool."

Lawson picks up a remote control that was just dropped off on stage by an assistant.

"You're going to love this. It's your very our remote controlled helicopter!"

The presenter flies the aircraft at full speed out towards the audience. One student flinches as it comes barreling right at him. Just when he thinks it's going to hit him, the helicopter pulls up in time to narrowly avoid the student's face. Once above him, the claw underneath the helicopter releases, dropping an uncooked turkey ball onto his lap. He shimmies around in his chair so it rolls onto the floor.

Lawson commands the helicopter to land on the ground next to him as he motions for Fields to change the slide. On the screen appears a close-up picture of the toy he just demonstrated where a miniature turkey wearing goggles can clearly be seen in the cockpit.

"Who knew turkeys could fly that well am I right?" Lawson comments with a grin. "Next slide please."

Fields changes the slide as directed.

"Here's where things get serious. We're at level G you guys and do you know what that means? It means G as in green. And it means green as in money. That's right, if you sell one-thousand boxes you not only get the turkey balls, and the keychain, and the mystery level C prize, and the football, and the t-shirt, and the helicopter, but you also get a one-hundred dollar bill."

He takes a one-hundred dollar bill out of his wallet and shows it off to the audience as if he thinks they've never seen one before.

"I've saved the second best for the second to last here folks. If you sell **five-thousand** boxes then you get to spend a day at Lawson Farms where we'll have a series of special activities planned for you that ends with a big party for everyone that reached that level."

He points to the slide that has only a stock photo of some balloons. He then points at Fields who changes to final slide.

"Finally we have level H. If you sell twenty-five thousand boxes of turkey balls then you'll get your very own Automated Personal Transport or A.P.T."

The slide shows a silver vehicle that looks like a large bucket with a seat big enough for one person and a touch screen attached to the inner rim in front of the seat.

"With the A.P.T., being lazy will never be easier. Just climb into the driver's seat and put on the helmet. Sensors in the helmet can detect the signals from your brain and will move the A.P.T. as if it were a part of you. There's also a touch screen if you'd rather use the manual controls or for connecting to the internet. No walking required. Ever. As a special bonus, we'll even include a Lawson Farms mascot decal so everyone will know who provided this awesome machine for you."

Principal Fields shuts off the projector and the screen gets retracted back to the ceiling.

"See? That's something to get excited about wasn't it? And all you've got to do is get out there and sell some turkey balls. Your teachers are passing out fliers with all the prize information, company information, and instructions for making a good salesman."

"Here you go, Grant. Here's your opportunity to prove how good of a salesman you really are." Curtis explains. "If you can sell twenty-five thousand of these things, no one will ever be able to doubt your ability again."

"Now I'm sure you'd all like to know what your raising this money for right?" Lawson continues. "You're not in this just for the prizes for yourself are you? No, of course you aren't. You want to help your school more am I right? Selling our product will be a big help and I'll tell you why. Your money will be going to…"

Rash crosses his fingers and wishes quietly.

"Come on, new pipes, new pipes, new pipes."

"Pay raises for your teachers! Minus the cooking and cleaning staff!" Lawson announces with a fist pump. "Yeah!"

"Damn it!" Rash outbursts. "I guess it's another year of bottled water for me."

"And I guess I'm going to have to start smuggling in my laptop if I want to get any kind of work done here." Parker adds. "Or earn one of those A.P.T.s."

"That's right. Without adequate pay, no teacher will have enough determination to be able to teach you properly. That's why you need to get out there and help your teachers help you by getting them the funding for the pay increases that they deserve."

Rash and Parker both boo him while Ace seems to be pleased with the cause.

"It's about damn time. I knew there had to be a reason why I was so stupid. Turns out that it's my teachers fault for not doing a good enough job at teaching. Figures."

The fliers reach Ace's group and he immediately checks to see what prize C is.

"It's a stuffed turkey. I don't know about you guys but I couldn't care less about most of this stuff. But I really want one of those A.P.T.s. And I want to help my teachers make me not stupid anymore."

"I'd like that as well." Parker comments.

"So we're all in agreement then? We're all going to do what we can to sell these right?" Ace wonders.

"If we're going to do that then why don't we make things a little more interesting?" Rash suggests. "We each have to pay fifty bucks to whoever sells the most out of the five of us."

"Agreed." They all say.

"Thanks for making me two-hundred dollars richer boys. Now there's just one more thing I got to know."

Ace shouts at Lawson as he walks off the stage.

"What do we get if we sell more than twenty-five thousand?"

"All the information you need is on the flier." He shouts back.

"Bitch, no it isn't. It only goes up to twenty-five thousand." Ace says loud enough for only his group to hear. "Do we just start getting the same prizes over again? I don't know. The mystery is really starting to scare me."

"Why are you even worried about that anyway?" Parker asks. "You don't stand a chance of making it that high. The only one of us that could even come remotely close to that quantity is me."

Ace crosses his arms and stares angrily at Parker.

"Oh yeah? Not if I have anything to say about it."

Chapter 3

After school, Ace rushes into the room the Randars are staying in at the Mann Hotel with Grant not far behind him, all the while waving around his flier. Marlena is lying in bed watching T.V. when she notices her two sons enter the room.

"Look what I've got! Look what I've got!" Ace excitedly announces.

His excitement dies down a little when he notices that his mother is the only one there to hear his news.

"Where is everybody? I need to share my exciting news with them."

"Working." Marlena answers using air quotes. "I put in my shift this morning, they've got the afternoon covered."

"That's too bad. I would've really liked them to be here for this but I can tell them later. My school's starting a fundraiser! We're raising money by selling turkey balls so we can pay our teachers more. Without proper pay, they won't be able to teach us good enough."

"You mean "well enough"." Marlena corrects.

"See? There you go. It's already happening."

"I don't know about that. That seems less like an example of poor teaching ability and more like a common mistake that you would make on purpose in order to try and prove your point."

"Nope. Bad teaching. We'd better hurry up and get them their money before things get even badder."

Marlena stares at her son in disbelief.

"Assuming you're as uneducated as you say you are, wouldn't the blame go to you for getting yourself suspended all these years? Your teachers can't teach you if you're not even there."

"This isn't about me." Ace whines. "This is about getting my teachers to start teaching me good."

"If you say so." Marlena sighs. "So what kind of garbage are we supposed to be selling anyway?"

"Turkey balls!"

"Balls? They're just meatballs made from turkey meat right? Not something else?"

"I don't know. It'll tell us right here on the sheet. Let's see."

He scans the paper until he finds the product information.

"Got it. It says they're made with one-hundred percent white meat turkey breast and other filler. Hmm, I guess it looks like there's no way of knowing what could actually be in there. Well nobody says we have to eat 'em. We just have to sell 'em. We get prizes if we sell them."

"Like what?" Marlena asks.

"Like this."

Ace shows his mother the picture of the A.P.T.

"You have to sell twenty-five thousand boxes to get that. That's never going to happen. Lawson Farm's has a bad reputation for health code violations and poor quality. Who's going to even want to buy something with their name on it?"

Ace crosses his arms in disgust.

"Ah, someone who cares about education and who wants to support a young man's dream of owning an A.P.T. Not like you. You're my mom and all you're doing is trying to crush my dream. A real mom would try and support my dreams no matter how impossible they are. But I guess you're not a real mom. Besides, this dream **is** possible because they also gave us a list of "dos" and "don'ts" for becoming a great salesman."

"Insults aside, I'm interested in hearing what kind of tips this list has for selling an immovable product. If exchange this for a better product isn't first on the list I'll be disappointed."

"Let's find out. I'll start with the "dos".

Do: go out alone. You can cover more ground if you split up.

Do: go out at night. More people are home at night.

Do: go to places you're not familiar with. If you don't know someone, then you don't know if they might want to buy a lot or not.

Do: buy plenty yourself. Who can you trust if not yourself?

Do: spend all day selling. No one likes a quitter."

"It wasn't there. What about the "don'ts"?"

"I'm getting there." Ace explains. "Here are the "don'ts.""

Don't: take no for an answer. Be persistent.

Don't: accept checks. Cash only

Don't: give away free samples. In life, you sometimes have to take risks.

Don't: leave home without your product. Opportunity knocks when you least expect it.

Don't: give refunds. What's done is done.

Don't: ask questions. Curiosity killed the cat.

And that's it."

"Wow. That's…troubling."

"It's going to be no trouble at all. I've got to sell twenty-five thousand and I've got to sell more than my friends. I have to!"

"And I have to sell more than Ace." Grant adds.

"No you don't. You could always lose instead." Ace retorts.

"That was all terrible advice. Your father and I will do our best to help you two in spite of that." Marlena informs. "I can't promise any more than that."

Chapter 4

Rash returns home to tell his parents about the fundraiser just as Ace is telling his.

"You're never going to believe this. The school's doing a fundraiser to help the teachers instead of the students."

Rash's dad guides him to a seat on the couch.

"Son, I believe that right now. Don't say that I'm never going to believe something that is so easily believable. It's **always** about money with them. You're never going to learn anything in that environment. I think it's about time that we got you away from all of those negative influences in that public school and we have me home school you instead. What do you say?"

"That's not where I was going with this at all." Rash counters. "I was just saying that I don't think that it would be the best use of the money, that's all."

"So you're not going to participate then?" Roland asks his son.

"Oh, I'm still going to participate. I have to. I made a bet with my friends that I'd sell the most."

"You mean your friends Ace and Grant?"

"Yep. And Curtis and Parker too."

"But Ace and Grant though? Oh, son, why'd you have to do that? Now I'm going to have to help you beat them."

"Or you could just let the boys have a little friendly competition." Delilah informs.

"Oh really? And do you think that Dirk and Marlena aren't going to try and help their kids win? Of course they will. That's why we have to beat them at all costs."

"Not at **all** costs. Mom's right. It's just a friendly wager. I still want to win though, but just in a kind and respectful manner."

"That sounds like something a loser would say. You're a Rash. That means you're a winner and winners don't lose no matter the cost. There's not a thing I won't do to beat the Randars. Alright, let's see what we're dealing with here." Roland orders.

"You can't see what we're dealing with right now. We pick up our boxes tomorrow. But I can just tell you what we're selling; it's balls of turkey meat."

"There have been tougher sells than that. I'll bring some boxes with me to work. It could get me fired, but it'll be worth it to beat the Randars."

"Don't get yourself fired." Delilah and Rash say together.

"I might. If that happens then I'll just have to become a full time turkey ball salesman. Long hours out on the road. Selling meatballs. The Randars realizing how inferior they are when they can't compete with me. I can't wait to see the looks on their faces when find out that they've lost to me."

"I shouldn't have said anything." Rash declares with a large amount of regret in his voice.

Roland walks over to the front door and swings it wide open.

"Well, no time to waste. I can't allow them to have a head start. It won't be enough just to win. I have to crush them every step of the way."

"But we don't even have the product yet! Or the order forms."

Roland ignores his son and walks out the door.

"Mom, aren't you going to do something about this?"

"No, it's best to just let him tire himself out. And who knows, he might even ending up selling a few boxes in the process."

At that moment, Roland steps back inside.

"I forgot my keys. That, and I also realized I was just doing something stupid. No one's going to buy something from me if they can't even see what I'm selling."

He strolls by his family to the kitchen with his head down in shame and without saying another word.

Delilah turns to her son.

"See?"

Chapter 5

The following day, minutes before school is to be let out, Ace and his friends, along with many others from the fifth grade class, are back in the auditorium to pick up their boxes of turkey balls and the folders to collect the money.

"So how many do we get?" Ace asks the Lawson Farms employee once he makes it to the front of the line.

"As many as you think you can sell." He answers.

"That many, huh? Let's just start with a hundred. I brought a wagon to haul them all in."

After the employee finishes loading all one hundred boxes onto the wagon, Ace turns around to face Rash who is next in line.

"So, Rash. Do you want to buy some turkey balls from me?"

"Why would I do that? I'm competing against you, remember?"

"So what is that then? A yes?"

"No."

"Then what is it?"

"It's a no."

"Really? I thought you were my best friend. Oh well."

"I **am** your best friend. I even died for you. So the least **you** could do to repay me is if you bought some turkey balls from **me**."

Ace groans and then kicks the wheel of his wagon in frustration.

"Fine. I'll buy one box."

"One? My life is only worth fifteen dollars to you? That hurts, man."

"You think your life is worth more than fifteen dollars? Get over yourself. Nobody's life is worth that much. But, just because I like you, I'll buy one more. As long as you buy one from me."

"Two more. And then I'll buy one from you." Rash offers.

"Deal."

The two friends shake hands on it and then exchange the money. Rash picks up twenty boxes from the employee and gives three to Ace who then gives one right back to Rash.

"First sale. Um um um um um yeah!" Ace cheers.

Rash and Ace leave the line allowing Grant, Parker, and Curtis to each pick up one hundred boxes a piece.

"I have this all figured out already." Parker informs. "You all might as well sit this one out and not even try."

"Nah, I think I'll try anyway." Ace responds.

"Shoot. So much for plan A. On to plan B then. I'll be seeing you all then…someplace."

Parker tows away his own wagon full of boxes while the rest of the group stays behind.

"I also have a plan." Curtis says. "I can't give away the details but it involves disregarding the "dos and don'ts" list entirely."

"Really?" Ace asks completely shocked. "I was going to follow that word for word."

"Neither of your plans will work." Grant states. "For you see, I have an advantage over all of you. I already have many regular customers. I'm going to dump all one hundred of these off on them today."

Grant laughs an evil laugh while his friends just stare blankly back at him.

"Good luck with that." Rash says as he walks off, heading for his father's car.

"I'd better be off to do my thing as well." Curtis announces before he exits the building too.

Ace looks at his wagon full of boxes and then at Grant.

"So what are we waiting for? Let's get out there and start selling already. And by us I mean me."

Ace runs as fast as he can with his wagon out into the parking lot. There he sees Rash approaching Miss Brick as she stands next to her car.

"How could you agree to this?" Rash asks his teacher. "Don't you know that the school needs things more than higher pay for you and your colleagues?"

"I didn't agree to it. I voted to use the money to replace all the carpets in the classrooms. One can only stand to see so many vomit stains before it makes you sick."

"Yeah, I'm like that too but with drinking lead. Which is why I wanted the pipes replaced."

"That option was suggested. But it only got a couple votes. The school nurse was, surprisingly, not one of them. She voted for the pay increase like many others. Apparently there hasn't been a pay raise in ten years."

"Oh. I didn't know that. Well that's not good."

"I wish I could have helped you, Rash, but there's just too many problems and not enough money to go around."

"I understand. Thanks for explaining everything."

Rash offers his hand to Miss Brick for a handshake when Ace comes storming out of nowhere and decks Rash in the jaw, dropping him to the ground.

"Ace!" Miss Brick exclaims.

"No. You're not going to sell to Miss Brick. I am."

"But he wasn't even trying to sell anything to me. We were just discussing how the funds would be used, that's all."

"He wasn't? Oops. My bad, dude."

Ace helps his friend to his feet just as he regains consciousness.

"Come on, man. You're taking this way too seriously." Rash says as he rubs his sore jaw.

"Shut up, Rash. So where were we? You're going to buy a half dozen boxes from me right, Miss Brick?" Ace asks. "I wouldn't eat them though. Unless you want to die."

"I wasn't going to buy from any student. It wouldn't be fair to buy from one and not the other. But with the way you just treated your supposed best friend, I think I'll buy two boxes from him after all."

"Thanks, Miss Brick!"

"You can't do that! I asked you, not him." Ace objects.

Miss Brick hands Rash the money and she accepts the two boxes.

"Just did it."

"Then buy some from me too. You have to. You just said you wanted it to be fair."

"It **is** fair. I'm compensating Rash for his pain and suffering on your behalf."

Miss Brick opens her car door and sits down in the driver's seat. Ace prevents her from shutting the door by holding on to it.

"Just one box. It's not going to hurt you."

"That's enough, Ace."

The teacher pulls on her door without enough force to break Ace's grip. However, her window is down so Ace shoves the flier up to her face through the opening and taps on number one of the "don'ts" list.

"I can't take no for an answer. The only way this is going to end is with you buying something from me."

Miss Brick backs out of her parking space and over the top of Ace's foot, causing him to hop around in pain.

"Sorry!" She calls back to him as she's about to pull out of the parking lot.

"You forgot something, bitch!"

Ace throws a box of his turkey balls at her car, causing it to burst open on the bumper. Miss Brick drives away as if nothing happened.

"Damn it. Rule number one sure as hell didn't work."

"In a way it did." Rash says as he walks up to Ace's side. "Now that you've opened that box, you have to pay for it. So it's a sale. Good job!"

Ace gives Rash a light push on the shoulder.

"**I** had to buy it though. Although, that **is** what they tell you to do on number four of the "dos" list. It's just that now you've sold five and I've only sold two. It's the first day and I'm already in the hole. I don't want to be in the hole. Get me out there!"

"You'd better get used to it. You're going to be in the hole throughout the entire competition." Rash taunts.

"Shut up."

Chapter 6

Cynthia Cromwell waits inside the old government building with her associates, Walker Ledford and Sheila Mathis.

"You know, I consider myself to be a very patient guy. But all we've been doing for the past few days is sitting around here doing nothing. Aren't we going to do something? Like use our superpowers to help people." Ledford asks.

"Yes we will." Cynthia answers. "Assuming Plat was able to accomplish my request."

"And what was this request exactly?" Mathis wonders. "Was it for him to abandon the team? Because that's sure what it seems like. He's been gone for days."

"That's to be expected, considering what my request was."

"Why's this request of yours such a secret anyway? Ledford inquires. "I thought we were a team?"

"It's not a secret. Everyone who was at the meeting the night we recruited Sheila knows about it."

"I wasn't at that meeting, though."

"Yeah, I know. Isn't it funny how that works? You thought it was a better idea for you to pretend like you didn't hear me and walk out the door when I told you I wanted to have a meeting than to actually show up for it."

"I did. But in my defense, I just assumed that Plat was going to blow it off too." Ledford argues.

"Well he didn't. And now his mission is a secret because there's no point to having meetings if we're just going to go over the information whenever."

"What about me?" Mathis asks. "I couldn't have gone to the meeting. I wasn't with the team yet."

"You'll all find out what Plat's mission is when he arrives."

At that moment, the Platinum Cyborg punches down the door to the conference room in which the members of S.U.P.E.R.P.O.W.E.R. were waiting.

"Like right now?" He asks.

"Hey, you just got here at the perfect time." Cynthia comments.

"Oh no I didn't. I've been here for a while. I was standing outside the door for some time waiting for the most dramatic moment to pop in."

"Oh. Well you still could have just **opened** the door."

"No I couldn't have. It was locked."

"I'm pretty sure it wasn't."

"Whatever."

Plat crouches down next to the table as there's no seat large enough for him. He sets the box he was carrying down next to him.

"I was out there abandoning my team when I thought to myself "I can't do this. I know what it's like to be on the other end of this." So I decided I'd do the secret assignment that Cynthia told me to do instead. I had my friend Pine make a couple dozen of the signal emitting watches you wanted and then distributed them to people just as you requested. Here's the bill he gave me."

Cynthia inspects the charges on the paper.

"What's this charge labeled "new uniforms" for? Did he make us new uniforms?"

"He did. At **my** request."

Plat takes one of the uniforms out of the box next to him and unfolds it so he can show it off to everybody.

"They're similar in design to the ones that we currently have except they have many more benefits such as greater resistance to projectiles, heat, and cold, particle filtering masks, shock absorbing boots, and that there's one for me."

"But wouldn't wearing this suit interfere with your ability to use some of your own weapons?" Cynthia wonders.

"Wouldn't **not** wearing this suit interfere with my ability to look like a part of the team? The answer is yes to both of our questions. But sometimes you just have to make sacrifices."

Ledford takes one of the watches out of the box and examines it more closely.

"So I assume people are supposed to turn on the signal when they're in trouble, right?"

Cynthia nods. "That's right. And then I'll teleport as many members of the team as necessary to stop the crime. We don't have enough people right now to patrol the streets as I would like so we have to do it this way first."

A light on the watch that Ledford is holding begins to blink.

"Uh-oh. Did I touch something that I wasn't supposed to?"

"Possibly. More than likely, though, it means someone is in trouble and is calling for our help. You and Sheila need to hurry up and get your new suits on while I look up the coordinates."

"What about me?" Plat asks. "Why don't I get to go?"

"Because I'd prefer to keep it at teams of two right now." Cynthia responds. "You can have the next one."

Plat crosses his arms and pretends to be upset.

"What if I don't want the next one?"

"What makes you think you want this one? This could be the worst incident we ever get. There's no way to know until you get there."

"Fine. I'll sit this one out. I just have more combat experience than the rest of you combined but I suppose that really doesn't mean anything."

"Great! Sheila? Walker? You guys ready?"

They both nod.

"Good. Be ready for anything."

"I don't know if that's actually possible." Ledford claims.

"Alright then. Be ready for as much as you can be." Cynthia corrects.

"We will."

Cynthia teleports the two of them off to their assignment as Plat takes the opportunity to make one last remark.

"That's why you should've sent me. I was built to be ready for anything."

Cynthia turns away from Plat and looks into the open doorway instead. There she sees Altes standing and watching them with great interest.

"I hope I'm not interrupting anything." He slyly says.

"Yes you do. You love to inconvenience others. Almost as much as you love being incompetent."

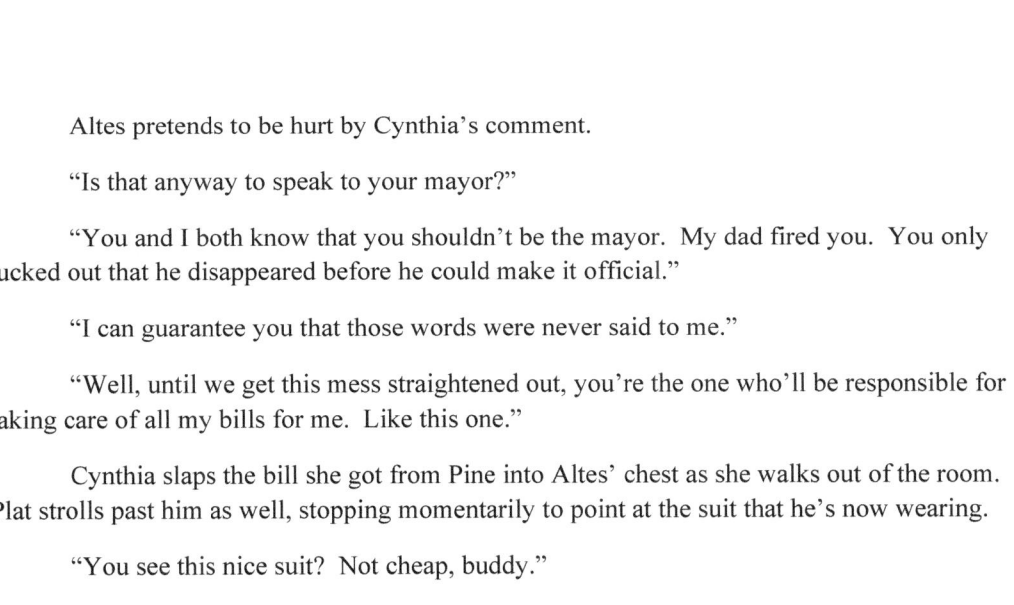

Altes pretends to be hurt by Cynthia's comment.

"Is that anyway to speak to your mayor?"

"You and I both know that you shouldn't be the mayor. My dad fired you. You only ucked out that he disappeared before he could make it official."

"I can guarantee you that those words were never said to me."

"Well, until we get this mess straightened out, you're the one who'll be responsible for aking care of all my bills for me. Like this one."

Cynthia slaps the bill she got from Pine into Altes' chest as she walks out of the room. Plat strolls past him as well, stopping momentarily to point at the suit that he's now wearing.

"You see this nice suit? Not cheap, buddy."

Chapter 7

Ledford and Mathis instantly appear in front of the person that activated the distress signal. The light on his watch continues to blink as Ledford charges a whip in each hand, getting ready for a fight.

"We're the members of S.U.P.E.R.P.O.W.E.R. you asked for." Mathis informs. "What's your emergency?"

"I accidentally bumped the button on the watch into a wall and now I can't get it to shut off. I think it's jammed."

Ledford's shoulders slump in disappointment as he retracts his whips.

"Are you kidding me? We thought you were in danger."

"I **am** in danger. I'm in danger of this flashing light annoying me to death." The man defends.

"I guess we'll have to take a look at it." Mathis says as she unlatches the watch from the man's wrist.

Both she and Ledford take a closer look at the watch and come to the conclusion that the button is in fact broken.

"You really did a number on this didn't you?" Ledford asks. "Were you intentionally smacking it against the wall or something?"

"No, I tripped on a plastic bag blowing in the wind. Which is really embarrassing now that I say it out loud."

"Yeah. It is. But don't worry about it. People will laugh at you and then move on. We don't have a replacement watch for you, though, so try not to get attacked until we can get this one fixed."

"That's going to be a problem. I'm actually expecting to get attacked this very night. The reason why I took one of the watches in the first place is because one by one the houses on my street have been getting broken in to. One house a night with each night it being the next house over. My house is next in line. I'm so scared! Please help me!"

"So stay out of your house tonight and you should be safe."

"But what about my stuff? I don't want it to get stolen."

"You should have thought about that before you got taken down by a bag."

"Also, we don't have anyone working the night shift." Mathis adds. "You were out of luck no matter what."

"Stop by the old government building in a day or two to see if we have your watch repaired. I don't know what else we can do for you at this time." Ledford concludes.

"You could always work overtime."

"We'll think about it."

Ledford and Mathis leave the man to find a secluded area where they can use their own watches to deliver their report to Cynthia.

"We've discovered an issue right off the bat." Ledford explains. "People can either hit the button accidentally or on purpose as a prank. The guy we found. He wasn't in trouble; he was clumsy. He broke his watch after tripping on a damn bag."

"Well that was five hundred dollars well spent. Do you think your friend can fix it, Plat?"

"Probably. Or he can just make a new one. It's not like they're irreplaceable and it's not like he has anything better to do. Government dollars have been spent on worse things, am I right?"

"I'm sorry; you're breaking up Plat. I think your watch might be broken too. I couldn't hear you after "probably"."

"We're in the same room, Cynthia; you could hear me just fine. For your information, I wasn't talking about your father's death fortress or his enforcer killing machines. I was talking about his salary and all the unnecessary construction projects."

Cynthia stares at Plat in a moment of awkward silence.

"Noted. Just get back here as soon as you can you two."

"No, wait a minute. Our light's blinking again."

Mathis looks at the coordinates for the emergency the light is signaling.

"That's right nearby here. We could be there in a minute."

"Go!" Cynthia orders before all four team members turn off the communication on their watches.

She looks back at Plat who's looking back at her.

"Well that got uncomfortable in a hurry."

Cynthia puts her head down a walks right out the front door.

Meanwhile, Mathis and Ledford rush to their next destination. Once they round the corner, they see a man with the light flashing on his watch looking quite distraught. He cheers up somewhat when he sees Sheila and Walker running towards him.

"We're the help you requested. What's the situation?" Ledford asks.

The man turns off the watch's signal and then gives Ledford a big hug.

"Oh, thank God you're here! It was so horrible! There I was, minding my own business, trying to buy a hot dog, when out of nowhere a quarter falls out of my pocket. I see it rolling towards the storm drain so I panic and hit the button but it was too late. It was gone! I had exact change only. I couldn't get my hot dog without that quarter!"

The man starts bawling into the shoulder of Ledford who is very annoyed by the situation.

"No way. This isn't real."

Walker tries to create some distance between himself and the man.

"Will you help me?" The man pitifully asks as he wipes away a tear.

Ledford pulls a quarter out of a pocket from the belt of his suit and tosses it to the man.

"There you go, dude. Problem solved."

"Thanks! Now can you get the other one for me?"

Walker looks over to Sheila for her opinion.

"I can't. The quarter isn't moving. I can't slow it down any more than that. My power's no help here."

"Neither is mine. My whips aren't magnetic or anything. I could melt it, probably, but not lift it."

"I just tried reaching my hand down there." Mathis informs. "It's out of arm's reach, that's for sure."

The man puts his hands on his head and shouts.

"What am I gonna do?"

"You're going to calm down and step back while you let us figure this out." Ledford commands.

The man quiets down as he takes a seat on the curb several feet away.

"We can do this. We've just got to put our heads together and figure this out."

"What if we put something sticky on the end of one of your whips? Like gum." Sheila suggests.

"That might work. Do you have any gum?"

"Nope."

"What about you, guy?"

The man shakes his head no.

"Alright then."

Ledford takes a trip to the nearest convenience store and returns with a pack of gum.

"Alright, I'm down a buck twenty-five right now. I'd have been better off just buying the guy his hot dog."

Walker looks around but can't see the man sitting anywhere.

"Where is he anyway?"

"He left." Mathis answers. "He decided to just use the quarter you gave him to buy the hot dog after all. Or he could've just pocketed it. I didn't actually see him spend it on anything but that's what he said he was going to do. Also, I have my doubts that the quarter was even his in the first place. I think he was just walking by and saw it lying there and thought we could get it for him."

Ledford dumps the pack of gum down the storm drain.

"Well, whatever the case, he's gone now. That means we don't have to waste any more time here. Too bad we couldn't take the watch from him first, though. Let's just get going."

Chapter 8

In the evening, Ace stands in the lobby of the Mann Hotel with the rest of his family, preparing to sell his collection of Lawson Farms turkey balls.

"Alright, it's night, I'm in a part of town I'm not familiar with, and I'm going to go out alone. I've got a good feeling about this."

"Are you sure you don't want me to come with you?" Marlena asks.

"Of course I'm sure! The instructions say to go out alone. Are you trying to sabotage me or something?"

"I know what the instructions say. I'm not the one who can't read, remember? It's just that I completely disagree with everything the instructions tell you to do."

"I've got to agree with your mother on this one." Dirk adds. "Criminals are more active at night. We don't want you to get hurt over some stupid contest."

"It's not a stupid contest. Our teachers need that money."

"I'm going out too." Grant declares. "I've informed my customers that my location has changed. And that my supplier's dead. I'm going to meet up with them a couple blocks down."

"Alright. Have fun!" Dirk tells his son.

Grant leaves as Ace's mouth hangs open in shock.

"What the hell? Why don't you have a problem with him going out?"

"Because he's one of the criminals."

"Well then I'm going out too. I don't even care. This fundraiser is the most important thing I'm ever going to do with my life and I'm not going to let you stop me from doing it."

Marlena sighs. "Unfortunately I believe that's all true."

Unaffected by his mother's comment, Ace pulls his wagon full of boxes out the door.

"Why's he bothering selling door-to-door anyway?" Dirk wonders. Wouldn't it be better to just make one large sale of the full twenty-five thousand units? It's what a smart person would do."

Marlena nods. "That's exactly what I was thinking."

She pulls out the coupon for a free dessert she got from Officer Gilbert and twirls it between her fingers.

"And I know the perfect place to do it."

"Me too. I was thinking about trying to sell them to this place for **their** restaurant. Or or their dumpsters. It doesn't matter to me what they do with them once they buy them."

While his parents continue to discuss their plans, Grant is out following through with his own. In an alley a couple blocks away, he slips his first customer the bag of drugs they purchased into their coat pocket along with a turkey ball.

"What was that?" The customer asks, referencing the ball.

"Shh. Just take it."

"But I don't even know what it was."

"It's good. You'll like it."

"Can I smoke it?"

Grant shrugs. "I don't see why not. In fact it would probably taste better that way."

"You've never let me down in the past, so I doubt you will today."

Grant pats him on the shoulder in an effort to encourage him to leave.

"I've get more people waiting. Hurry along now."

Grant continues to give out a free turkey ball with each deal he makes, causing concern to one customer who questions him about it.

"Why are you giving us raw meat, man? That's disgusting."

"I'm branching out. I stuffed yours full of pot, so I'd quit complaining if I were you. I'd quit complaining if I were all of you! This is a sweet deal you're getting."

"Oh. Thanks."

That customer leaves satisfied as do the remaining few after him. In all, Grant gives out twenty free samples, enough to make **him** satisfied with the days work.

Meanwhile, Ace is out testing his own strategy. He stops at each home he comes across, ringing the doorbell several times before moving on once nobody answers. The people who do answer immediately tell him "no thanks" and shut the door before he can argue. Frustrated, he stops at a street corner to rethink his strategy.

"Why don't people want to support this great cause? I either need to offer them something they're guaranteed to want first or I need to make the sales pitch someplace they can't easily escape from. Okay, I've got a plan; let's see how this works."

After several tries, Ace finds a homeowner who answers the door.

"Hello?"

"Hi! Would you like me to give you five free dollars?"

"I would like that. What's the catch?"

"There's no catch. All you have to do support Mann Elementary School by buying a box of delicious Lawson Farms turkey balls for fifteen dollars each. It'll go to a great cause."

"Lawson Farms huh? I've heard bad things about them. No thank you."

The home owner is about to close the door when Ace stops them.

"Wait! I've got one more thing you might be interested in."

"And what's that?"

"A ticket to hell, you jerk. That's where you're going for not supporting this great cause!"

The person closes the door in the middle of Ace's yelling.

"So much for that."

Ace runs to the space in between this house and the one next to it. There he notices that a window is open on the side of the neighboring home and so he climbs right in. All of the lights are off, so Ace turns on a flashlight allowing him to navigate his way to the owner's bedroom. Once inside the room, he closes the door and tip-toes right next to the man's bed. He taps the man on the shoulder until he wakes up.

"Hey, do you want to buy some turkey balls?" He whispers.

Startled, the man rolls out of the other end of the bed and picks up a crowbar he keeps underneath it.

"What the hell are you doing in here?"

"I'm supporting a great cause. And so could you. All you have to do is buy a box of turkey balls or two."

"Get outta here!"

The man charges Ace with the crowbar. Ace throws the box of turkey ball at man, hitting him in the face. He then jumps out of the second story window and limps away with his wagon.

"I hate you "dos" and "don'ts" list! You've brought me nothing but pain."

He crumples the list into a ball and blindly tosses it away, hitting his classmate Dean as he was walking along the sidewalk towards him.

"Ace! What are you doing here?"

"Not selling anything, that's for sure."

Dean takes off then unzips the backpack he was wearing to show Ace that it's filled with boxes of turkey balls.

"Same here. But I live in this neighborhood. So this is **my** turf. If anyone's going to not sell anything here, it's me. Actually, now that I think of it, I never did thank you for sneaking glue into my vanilla pudding yesterday." He says sarcastically.

"Oh you don't have to thank me for that." Ace replies. "I was only doing that to be mean."

"Oh? So you'll understand why I have to do this then."

Dean tips over Ace's wagon and stomps on several boxes, while kicking several others out of the way. Ace can only stand and watch in horror.

"No chance for you to sell anything now, ass!" Dean shouts as he runs off.

"Jokes on you, bitch; I'm going to try and sell them anyway." Ace yells back.

He looks down at the boxes trashed and scattered all over a stranger's front lawn.

"What a mess."

Chapter 9

Walker and Sheila are back at their headquarters with Cynthia and Plat for an evening meeting.

"First off, I'd like to thank Walker for showing up to this one. These meetings are important you guys; we've got to take them seriously." Cynthia announces.

"I'd like to thank the Platinum Cyborg for showing up to the first one." Plat adds. "Let's all say it together. I'd like to thank the Platinum Cyborg for…"

"I already thanked you once." Cynthia interjects. "That should be enough."

"It would be if my ego weren't so large."

"Thanks again, Plat. Now let's get on to the reason why I called this meeting. Today was our first time sending people out into the field and our first time using the watches. I need to how this went and I'd like to know where we need to improve."

"People were constantly pranking us." Ledford states with a little edge in his voice. "Not one person we were called to today needed our help. For real. As in their lives weren't actually in danger. I mean, the final one of the day only called us there to see if the button actually worked."

"Well not the first guy." Mathis corrects. "I think he was actually going to need our help. It's just that he broke his watch and he needed it at night. Which brings me to a suggestion I'd like to make. We should hire someone to work at night."

"I was planning on doing some more recruiting tomorrow." Cynthia informs.

"Well can you get someone who can either teleport or fly us around?" Walker asks. "You can get us to our first location quickly but then we have to walk the rest of the way. There's no way we'll be able to get to people in time that way."

"Here's the thing. My plan is for there to be multiple teams of two out patrolling different parts of the city at all times. The nearest team to the signal responds to it. Unless there's no one close. Then I'll send a reserve team from here directly to the location who will then return here once the assignment's complete."

"So what you're saying is that until we get enough teammates, people are just going to have to hope that we happen to be in the area when they need help?"

"Yep."

"Or you could get some thrusters installed in your feet like me." Plat suggests. "That'll get you back here quick."

"Installed? I thought you were born with those there." Cynthia says with a wink.

"I was." He answers, having taken the hint. "But I'm just saying that if you weren't born with the same hideous deformity that I was you could get it done to yourself. My friend Pine's very good at it."

"That's great. Does anyone have any more suggestions or concerns?"

"Yeah, Walker mentioned something interesting earlier today. If someone uses their watch as a prank, do we have the right to take it from them?" Mathis wonders.

"Why don't we start by giving them a warning first? If they do it again then you can take it from them."

"And then if they don't want to give it back you have the right to beat the hell out of 'em." Plat adds.

"No. You don't." Cynthia corrects. "We just stop responding to their signal."

"Yeah, and then that idiot gets to keep a five hundred dollar watch for being an idiot. Right. Like that's fair."

"But you **are** telling us to ignore a distress signal then, aren't you?" Sheila asks.

"If you constantly use your watch inappropriately? Then yes, you'll be ignored."

"But what if they actually need our help and we don't show up? Their life goes: prank, prank, prank, held up at gun point, oops I actually need saving now; I guess I shouldn't have pranked those people so many times, now I'm dead."

"That's right. They shouldn't have pranked us. They broke our trust and now they have to deal with the consequences. I never said this was a perfect system but it's the best we can do without monitoring people twenty-four seven. Which we can all agree that no one wants anyway."

"You're not giving yourself enough credit." Plat tells Cynthia. "This **is** a perfect plan and we'll all do our best to make sure that there'll be no such thing as criminals anymore. Am I right guys?"

The Platinum Cyborg raises both of his hands so Walker and Sheila can give him a high-five, which they do.

"That's right! Although, not having someone working at night is still a serious issue. I'd bet fifty dollars' worth of my pinky finger that that first guy is getting his house ransacked right now."

Cynthia sighs. "Yeah. Probably. We just have to accept that this problem won't be fixed overnight. Great meeting everyone. You can all go home now. I'll be staying here because this **is** my home now."

Chapter 10

In the morning, the Randars gather in the lobby of the Mann Hotel with Ace being the last to arrive. He walks in towing his wagon full of smashed boxes behind him.

"Well, I'm off to go selling. See you guys whenever."

Marlena stops him before he can go out the door.

"Wait just one moment. Today's a school day. You can't just skip school to sell turkey balls."

"Watch me."

"Watch you get on the bus to go to school? Gladly."

"No, watch me skip school."

Marlena picks up one of the smashed boxes and takes a closer look at its contents.

"What happened to these? Have you even been refrigerating them?"

"They don't have to be refrigerated." Ace answers.

"But it says "keep refrigerated" right on the box."

"Geez, no one's pointing a gun to my head and forcing me to refrigerate them. Damn."

"Fine. Do things your way. I'm just trying to save you some trouble since your dad and already have this figured out for you."

"I've got this figured out as well." Grant boasts. "I handed out some free samples to my customers last night. They should be coming to me begging for more anytime now."

"You handed out free samples?" Ace asks. "The instructions say not to do that."

"I don't care what the instructions say. Giving away free samples is how you get people hooked on your product. I've been doing it for years."

"That only works if the product you're giving away is any good, Grant." Marlena informs. "Once your customers try these turkey balls they'll never want to buy a whole box from you."

"Oh, we'll see about that. Let's just see what they're saying about me on Dealr. I've probably got a couple dozen sale requests waiting for me."

Grant takes out his phone to look up his profile and is shocked by what he sees.

"**My Dealr rating went down**! Look at all these two and three star reviews. "Started selling awful meat product. DO NOT BUY! It made me sick. Two stars." "Gave me raw meat that I didn't ask for. Spent whole night on toilet…and on ecstasy. Three stars." "New product failed to give me a high. Two stars." **What is wrong with these people**? **I'm ruined!**"

Ace cracks his fingers together with a huge grin on his face.

"Well, looks like you're out of the competition."

"Oh no he isn't." Dirk disagrees. "I'm going to be making a sales pitch for Grant later today. It'll be fair because your mom will be doing one for you at the same time. Neither of you have to worry about anything. We'll both get you your twenty-five thousand easily."

"Just make sure you get me twenty-five thousand and one, mom. I've got to come in ahead of Grant." Ace explains.

"Well then you're going to have to get me twenty-five thousand and two, dad." Grant counters.

"You'd better watch it, Grant. Don't make me go to twenty-five thousand and three." Ace warns. "I'll do it."

Now it's Grant's turn to have the smug look on his face.

"I think I just did."

Marlena shakes her head at the two of them.

"This is getting silly. You're both getting twenty five and we'll call it even."

"But what if Rash gets more than that?"

"Well then you lose. That's how competitions work." Dirk points out.

"But I don't want to lose."

Dirk shrugs. "Tough."

"Now go to school so your parents can do your work for you." Ace's mother orders.

Chapter 11

Parker stands outside the Lightbot Mini-mart just before it opens, waiting to meet with its owner, one of the robots known as lightbots. The lightbots' heads consist of three glass cylinders separated by thin metal disks. Each cylinder lights up as a different traffic light color since they were built to serve as traffic lights. However, due to a programming error, some of them became shopkeepers instead. The store owner, Lightbot GR1, opens the front door to its business, with Parker immediately waking inside before the door is even opened all the way.

"I hope no one has come to you yet about buying these."

Parker hands the robot a box of turkey balls. It forms an expression as close to confusion as something without a face possibly can. It then responds by making a series of dinging noises accompanied by flashes of different colored light.

"I'll take that as a no. Well then do I have quite an offer for you? How would you like to be an honored retailer of Lawson Farms turkey balls? A first time purchase of fifty-thousand units is all it takes."

The robot flashes the red light only while dinging in a deeper tone, meaning it's angry. A piece of paper with its translated words on it prints out of a slot on its chest. GR1 hands it to Parker who reads it out loud.

"*You must think I'm some sort of idiot. Lawson Farms was responsible for that bird flu outbreak a couple years back. I can't have my brand attached to that.* That's actually not true. It was only strongly suspected that they were responsible for the outbreak. No concrete evidence was ever found."

The light bot crosses its arms and makes dinging noises that make it sound like it's skeptical of Parker's explanation. It prints another sheet of paper to fully translate.

"*Why would I take that risk though?* I'll tell you why. These are the best meatballs you'll ever taste."

The lightbot slowly rotates its head back and forth, then hands Parker another sheet of paper.

"*I can't taste.* I didn't mean you specifically; I meant you in a general sense."

GR1 shakes its head again while all three parts of its head are now glowing red.

"*No, you meant me specifically.* How do you know what I meant? *I just do.*"

Parker crumples the sheet of paper causing GR1's head to glow bright yellow in shock.

"How dare you crush my words before me? You'll get no sale from me!"

The lightbot walks back behind the register with Parker following it there.

"You have to reconsider. What if I told you that a small portion of the proceeds will be going to help local schools? Would that change your mind?"

GR1 prints another sheet of paper in response.

"I don't have any children in any school so no it would not. Then just do it out of the goodness of your heart. *I don't have a heart."*

Parker crumples the last sheet of paper he was given and throws it into the trash.

"Why do you have to take things so literally? I'd like to meet the person who programmed you so I can teach him how to properly program a robot meant for human interaction."

GR1's head glows bright red while it makes a continuous, high pitched whistle. Paper streams out of its chest with the word "security" printed repeatedly all over it.

"That won't be necessary."

Parker turns to run but two more lightbots swoop in and grab him. At that moment, GR1's head switches to bright green, signifying joy. It then prints the word "yes" repeatedly.

The two lighbot security guards toss Parker outside. One of them drops a note on top of him as he lies on his back in the parking lot.

"Don't mess with the lightbots...ever."

From his position on the ground, Parker can see the lightbots inside congratulating each other with an excessive amount of high-fives, handshakes, and hugs.

"That definitely didn't go the way I expected. Perhaps a human store owner will be more reasonable."

Parker checks the time and sees that it's only five minutes before the start of school.

"I'll revisit this matter later."

Chapter 12

At noon, Officer Gilbert hangs a plaque on the wall in the entryway of the Best Restaurant Ever. He looks over his shoulder to see Officer Summers standing right behind him.

"Whoa, you scared me there. What are you doing standing so close behind me?"

"Wondering why you're redecorating without consulting me, your boss, about it first."

"I wanted it to be a surprise for you. We just received this very prestigious award in the mail today. We were named number one new restaurant by Diarrhea Enthusiast Magazine."

"Ugh, why would you hang **that** up on the wall? That's not something good. That you would actually do that **is** a surprise, just like you wanted."

"It doesn't matter who it's from. People are going to see the big shiny number one and not care about any of what's written underneath it." Gilbert defends.

"You'd better be right. Our first customer is here."

Summers tries to compose himself as Marlena enters the building. Gilbert is delighted to see her.

"Hey! Welcome to the Best Restaurant Ever! I'm so glad you decided to give us another try. Where's the rest of your family?"

"At school, working, pretending to be working, or any combination of the three. Whatever the case is they won't be joining us. I only have the coupon for the one free dessert after all."

Marlena looks over and reads the plaque.

"Number one by Diarrhea Enthusiast? Ouch. I would **not** be proud of that."

Summers immediately takes the plaque down after hearing that.

"We're not. I have no idea why they gave us that."

"Your customers definitely do." Marlena comments. "But enough of the small talk. I actually have a bit of business I'd like to discuss with you."

"Business?" Gilbert asks. "What kind of business?"

"The kind where I try to sell you something."

She gives her coupon to Summers.

"Here, I'll take my free dessert and then we can sit down and talk about it."

Summers leaves for the kitchen as Gilbert escorts Marlena to a table where they sit across from each other.

"So what are you trying to sell us?"

"You guys like salmonella and E.coli and all that right?"

"More like **it** likes **us** but go on."

"Well if you'd like to keep getting more plaques like the one I just saw then you'll definitely want to buy some Lawson Farms turkey balls from me. Just twenty-five thousand and five boxes is all it's going to take."

Gilbert taps his chin in thought.

"Hmm, Lawson Farms. That sounds familiar. It must be because it was the name on that load of boxes we just bought from Powell's kid. You'll notice that the majority of our menu now consists of dishes made with turkey balls because of it. That's including drinks and desserts."

Summers joins them at the table without Marlena's free dessert.

"It appears that the coupon for the free dessert you gave me is only valid with the purchase of an entrée. Would you like to do that?"

Marlena glares at Gilbert.

"You son of a bitch. You weren't trying to make things up to me at all. You were just trying to trick me into buying something that I didn't really want. Who does that? Speaking of which, I assume it's a no then to the turkey balls?"

"Once we get though the twenty-five thousand we already bought you'll be the first person we call." Gilbert explains.

"By then it'll be too late. And this trip turned out to be quite the waste of time. I was going to take down my poor review of this place if you had decided to buy from me but I think I'll just add another one instead. Not that it needs any more negative reviews that is."

Marlena gets up, throws the coupon into the fountain, and then walks out the door.

Chapter 13

Phinn, Ginn, and Dinn stand in the street in front of the Randar's place as a construction crew works on rebuilding it.

"Are you sure this is the right place?" Ginn asks. "It doesn't look like anyone's living in here right now."

Phinn nods. "Yes. I can tell by all the damage I did to it."

"Alright then."

Ginn rolls into the construction site and starts tosses around the workers. He holds on to one so he can punch them multiple times in the face.

"This is what you get for hurting my little brother!"

Phinn rushes to Ginn's side to prevent him from hurting the person any further.

"No! These aren't the humans we have a problem with."

"Are you sure?" Dinn asks. "They're destroying all the work you did to bring down this building by rebuilding it."

"That's okay. I can level a building anytime I want to and people will still be impressed by it. But hurting a random human won't have an effect on the humans I want to hurt."

"Is that true?" Ginn wonders. "Maybe I just haven't hurt him badly enough yet."

"It's true."

Ginn lets the construction worker go allowing him to run over to his coworkers who were watching the whole thing a few feet away. He then hits the button on the watch given to him by S.U.P.E.R.P.O.W.E.R.

"You actually used that thing? That's so embarrassing." One coworker taunts.

Walker and Sheila appear in uniform right in front of them.

"We're the representatives from S.U.P.E.R.P.O.W.E.R. you asked for. If this is a prank tell me now because if I find out after the fact I'll be a lot angrier." Ledford informs.

Mathis looks around and notices all the injured construction workers lying on the ground.

"Whoa! I don't think this is a prank. I think someone really did just beat up all these guys. They're even moaning and everything."

Walker comes face to face with the guy who summoned him.

"These guys aren't just pretending to be hurt, are they?"

He shakes his head. "No this is real. The culprit is standing behind you. It's that light blue dolphin in the middle. The other two are innocent as far as I know."

Walker turns around to face the dolphins who are all surprised to see that he and Sheila showed up.

"Alright then. Let's do this."

He extends a whip from each hand and immediately begins charging them. Phinn cordially waves back at him.

"Excuse me, human? It looks like your intestines just slipped out of your hands. You might want to take care of that."

He leans over to whisper to Ginn.

"That is what they are right? Human organs glow bright orange, don't they?"

Ginn shrugs. "I don't think so. Those must be something else."

Walker smacks Phinn across his face with one of the whips, leaving a slight burn.

"Ew, he hit me with it!" Phinn says as he rubs the burn. "But I'm going to let that one slide since I assume you were aiming for Ginn but missed. If you hit me again though, then it's go time."

"Go for it. Stay close to me and I'll protect you from whatever they can throw at you." Sheila informs.

Walker nods and then hits both Phinn and Ginn in their midsections with Dinn avoiding the blow by standing a couple feet behind his brothers.

"That's it human! You involved yourself in something that doesn't concern you so I gave you the chance to leave. But you should know that I can't stand to be whipped."

Phinn fires an energy beam at Ledford that gets caught in Mathis' slowing field and dissipates harmlessly leading to more confusion for Phinn.

"What? Usually when I do that the human blows up right away. I don't what happened."

"Maybe it's because you didn't try hard enough." Ginn suggests.

"Uh-oh. You noticed that? I guess I'll try harder this time."

Phinn launches an even larger energy beam but it produces the same effect as the first one.

"That was the best I could do."

Ginn gently pushes Phinn behind him.

"Step aside little brother. It's time for a real man to go to work."

Ginn shoots one of his own energy beams at Sheila and Walker but again it does nothing.

"That didn't work either! Time to flee!"

Ledford wraps a whip around Phinn and Ginn, tripping them both as they try to run away.

"Eek! He's got me!" Phinn squeals.

Dinn laughs at his brothers. "It's a good thing he doesn't have three of them or I would've gotten caught too. Later!"

Ginn shouts at Dinn as he rolls away.

"Get back here and help us!"

"Good luck!" He shouts back.

Walker tries pulling the dolphins in towards him but isn't able to make any progress.

"It's no good. They're just too damn heavy. We need Plat."

Sheila contacts Cynthia with her watch.

"Are you there, Vanisher? We need you to send us the Platinum Cyborg. We actually have some real criminals apprehended but we need a little extra muscle."

"*Lucky for you I'm a **lot** of extra muscle*." Plat brags.

"Can you get him here?"

Phinn and Ginn try rolling away so Sheila let's go of Walker's shoulder causing him to become affected by the slowing field, effectively making him an anchor.

"This isn't working!" Phinn complains.

"*I don't really like the idea of leaving any one of us alone*." Cynthia answers.

"It'll only be for a minute." Sheila pleads. "And then for however long it takes for us to get back. So it could be a while actually."

"*Fine.*"

Cynthia teleports the Platinum Cyborg next to Mathis just as Phinn and Ginn each use their energy beams to snap each other's restraints and roll away. Before lowering her field, Sheila has Plat hold Walker in place.

"Well this is great timing. I got here just in time to watch them escape." Plat says. "And what a sight it is. Such beautiful creatures they are. I could try and hit them with a rocket quick if you want me to."

"*Do you have a clear shot?*" Cynthia asks.

"No. There's a bunch of kids running around down there."

"*Then don't risk it.*"

Plat keeps his arm pointed at the dolphins until they're out of sight. He then keeps it raised for a couple seconds afterwards.

"I could've probably made that shot. Now we'll never know." Plat sorrowfully states.

"Cheer up. We saved this guy and all his coworkers from further suffering. And that's all that really matters." Sheila declares.

"Is it though?" The cyborg asks. "Who is this guy? He's nobody. Who cares what happens to him. But if we keep letting all the criminals escape, we'll never get the respect we deserve."

"I'm going to pretend I didn't hear that." Mathis tells him.

"Just as well. I'm going to pretend that I didn't say it."

Walker pats the guy they saved on the back.

"Stay safe, man. But if you don't, feel free to call us anytime. Nine A.M. to eight P.M. only. Monday thru Friday."

"Will do. Thanks again for rescuing me. I don't know why those dolphins went after us like they did."

"It was obviously because beating up people is fun." Plat declares. "What other reason do they need than that?"

"Left your filter at home today, did you?" Ledford asks in an attempt to persuade Plat into being more selective with his comments.

"Nope. That's just how I live my life. Unfiltered like the city's tap water. I say whatever comes to mind."

"*Not if you want to keep your job you don't.*" Cynthia admonishes him through Sheila's watch.

"Is that still on? Here, let me turn that off for you."

Plat tries to shut off Mathis' watch but his fingers are too large to hit the button so he gives up. The whole situation has made the construction workers uncomfortable.

"I think we're going to get back to work. We don't need another client complaining about us not us getting the work done in the time that we estimate. Five times is enough already."

"We should probably get back to work too." Sheila announces. "It's a long walk back. It's not getting any shorter by standing around."

"You know, I have a way to get back that's much faster than walking." The Platinum Cyborg boasts.

"So what are you waiting for? Let's see it." Ledford encourages.

Plat calls a cab and the three members of S.U.P.E.R.P.O.W.E.R. ride it all the way back to the old government building. Walker isn't the least bit impressed.

"I thought you meant something else."

Chapter 14

Cedrick Adler arrives back at the Mann Hotel after his lunch break and stops at the front desk to drop his trash in the waste basket nearby when Dirk pops up from behind the counter.

"Boo!"

Adler jumps up and grabs his chest in shock.

"What are you doing, Randar? You know I don't like surprises."

"I know. Me neither. I don't know why I did that. But now that we're on the subject of surprises, I've got another surprise for you. One of the pleasant variety this time."

Dirk lifts a box of turkey balls from underneath the counter and drops them in front of Adler.

"Boom! It's a box of high quality turkey meat. I bet the hotel's restaurant would love to get a hold of twenty-five thousand and five boxes of these. They'll be the talk of the town."

"Will the town be saying good things?"

"Things." Dirk evades.

Adler slides the box back to Dirk.

"I'd love to help you but now isn't a good time. Rich Mann is going to be here shortly to discuss the budget with me. I don't think it's wise to be adding another massive charge on there until he leaves."

"Rich Mann is coming? Why didn't you warn me sooner?"

Adler shrugs. "Surprise."

"No. If he knows I've been siphoning off funds from him, I'm ruined."

Dirk speaks into his communication device to warn his employees.

"Attention members of Backfire. We have a code green. I repeat this is a code green. Lock yourselves in your rooms or another secure hiding place until further notice."

At that moment the front door begins to open and Dirk spots Mann as the one opening it.

"Oh no!"

He draws his rappel gun and shoots it into the ceiling. Dirk then hoists himself to the top and tries to hide behind a chandelier.

Rich Mann charges into the room and straight for Adler after Dirk is out of sight.

"Good. You're here. I'll cut right to the chase then. One of my accountants noticed a dramatic increase in the spending for towels. Care to explain that, Mr. Adler?"

"People like to steal towels from hotels. There's nothing new about that."

"I'm aware of that. What I'm saying is that it appears that people are starting to steal six times as many more towels as they used to. Either that or you're embezzling money from me."

"I'd never do that, sir. But maybe I could hire some security to help cut down on this towel theft?" Adler suggests.

"Maybe I could fire you and bring in someone else who can keep a tighter grip on things here?"

"That won't be necessary. I'll tighten my grip; I promise."

"No, I'm definitely firing you. Whether you're stealing money from me or just letting someone else do it, there's no reason to keep someone that incompetent around."

At that moment, the chandelier Dirk is hiding behind falls to the ground, shattering just a couple feet behind Mann. He looks up to see where the chandelier fell from but Dirk has already rappelled down to him.

"Your chandelier was a little loose. You're lucky that didn't fall on somebody or their family would end up owning this place."

Mann points an accusing finger at Dirk.

"I remember you. I hired you to protect my art collection not too long ago. How'd that go again?"

"How would I know? I don't remember the jobs that end poorly."

"So what are you doing here besides breaking more of my works of art?" Mann asks.

"I came here, to present you with an exciting business opportunity."

"Not interested."

"You don't even know what I was going to say." Dirk tries to reason.

"I meant I'm not interested in hearing you talk to me anymore. Whatever words you planned on speaking are irrelevant. My business here is concluded. Unless you want me to call my enforcers in here and have them rough you up for damaging my property?"

"Not particularly."

"Oh well. I was hoping I'd get to enjoy watching you take your punishment but since you don't want it I guess there's nothing I can do."

"I guess not." Dirk says flatly.

Mann shakes his head and laughs. "Except that's not how it works, idiot."

He then whistles loudly causing two enforcers to come jogging to his side in response to his call.

"Get him boys."

Dirk tries to run away but the enforcers immediately catch him and fling him to the ground where they repeatedly kick him in the ribs.

"A thought has occurred to me. This man works security. Mr. Adler, you said you wanted to hire some security. Were you trying to trick me into hiring this man and his team again?"

Adler shifts around uncomfortably.

"No."

"Don't lie to me, Mr. Adler. See what's happening to him? You don't want a part of that do you?"

"No, I'm telling you the truth. I wasn't trying to trick you into hiring him. I was planning on hiring him without you knowing about it."

"That's worse. Boys!"

Mann flicks his finger from the enforcers to Adler, indicating he wants them to go after **him** now. Adler doesn't even try to run; he just stands there and takes his punches with a look of utter defeat on his face. He drops to the floor next to Dirk once his beating is done."

"I think you guys just learned your lesson."

Mann turns to walk away but Dirk reaches out and stops him by grabbing on to his foot.

"Wait." He says weakly. "Don't you want to buy some turkey balls from me? It's for charity."

Mann orders his enforcer to kick Dirk one more time, causing him to let go of his foot. He then stops just as he's about to step out the door.

"Edgar Hopkins, the assistant manager will be promoted to your position, effective immediately. He'll help you two out of the building."

"I think the assistant manager's still a golem, isn't he?" Adler whispers to Dirk.

"I think that's not our problem anymore." Dirk whispers back.

Chapter 15

Roland Rash struts into the breakroom of the office where he works. It's his turn to bring treats in for the office so everyone is excited to see him.

"Alright! Roland's here. What'd you bring us?"

"Ooh, did I bring you guys something good or what? You guys are really going to love this. Close your eyes."

His coworkers all do as they're told as he sets an open box of turkey balls on the table in front of them.

"Alright, you can open them now."

The expressions on all of Roland's coworkers' faces turn from excitement to a combination of anger and confusion.

"What the hell is this, Roland? Is this some kind of joke?" One asks.

"These are some awfully funny looking donuts." Comments another. "Not to mention smelly."

"I'm not bringing donuts. I thought you guys would like to try something different."

"You thought wrong, my friend." Another coworker scoffs.

"Okay. Well if you don't want to try them then maybe you just want to buy a box or two for yourself."

Several people have already left the room to go and get their own snack while a couple people remain to further criticize Roland.

"Guy, I already had to buy fifty of these stupid things to get my kid that stuffed turkey. I tried donating them to a homeless shelter afterwards but they refused them saying that it was better to be homeless than dead."

"Yeah, aren't these contaminated with bird flu or something?" His coworker Sonya asks.

"That was a couple years ago; don't they deserve a second chance?" Roland replies.

"Probably. But I'll leave it up to someone else to give it to them." She says as she leaves the room.

Roland closes the door behind her and then turns to face his last remaining coworker.

"It's just you and me, John. Are you going to buy some turkey balls or am I going to have to report you to H.R. for all the times you've taken your lunchbreaks on the clock?"

"You wouldn't dare." John replies while staring back intensely.

"I've done worse to people over less." Roland informs.

"Well then I'll report you for locking me in the breakroom and harassing me."

"Well played."

Roland takes the box of turkey balls and exits the breakroom, leaving the door open. He comes back in a minute later to post at note that reads: *See Roland for exciting news.* Soon afterwards, someone writes the word "don't" at the start of the note.

Roland spends the next couple of hours expecting people to come to him for sales but none do. That's when he decides to print out a sign-up sheet instead. Roland takes the sheet into the breakroom and pins it next to his previous note. He immediately notices the change that was made to the first note and becomes furious.

"Alright, who did this?" He shouts. "**Who**?"

"We all assumed you did it." Sonya answers for the group.

"Yes, I made the note. But then someone changed it to mean the opposite of what I intended and I want to know who!"

Roland throws a stapler into the far end of the office, putting a small hole into the wall.

"The culprit definitely isn't going to fess up now after seeing an attitude like that."

"Fine. You know what? Since whoever did this likes writing notes so much, I'll leave a note where they can put their confession on. If you just admit it, I won't get mad and we can put this all behind us."

Roland returns to the breakroom and writes another note that leaves an empty space for the person to write their name followed by the words "did it". He then goes back to his desk and works until a couple minutes before the end of the day when he gets up to check on the note. An arrow pointing up to the words "not do" has been drawn in between "did" and "it". Already angry, Roland looks to see if anyone placed any orders on his sign-up sheet. He sees the name "N. Obody" with a zero next it to it and no other names. This sends him into a rage.

"**What kind of person thinks this is funny?**"

Roland rips the bulletin board off the wall and hurls it into the wall behind him. He then proceeds to the flip over every chair and table in the room. He comes out of the room with his box of turkey balls as every else starts to get up and leave.

"Hey guys, I know you think playing jokes on me is funny so maybe you'd like it if I played a little joke on all of you for a change?"

Roland slowly dumps all of the turkey balls out of the box and into the trash.

"It's a three day weekend, everybody. You know this isn't going to smell good once you get back."

His coworkers ignore him as they all walk past him and out the door. Once everyone else is gone, Roland leaves the office as well. When he gets home, he is immediately questioned by his son.

"Did you sell a ton of boxes for me, Dad?"

Not wanting to disappoint Rash, Roland goes against his better judgment and lies.

"Absolutely. You'll win your bet for sure."

Chapter 16

Ace is in the lunch line with his friends. In his hands, he carries a smashed box of turkey balls with a tag reading "one dollar each" on it. As he nears the end of the line, Ace sets the open box on top of the mini carrots and then pays for his meal. He then sits down with his friends at their usual table.

"I can't believe that no one else thought of that before me." Ace declares.

"Oh they've thought of it alright. They thought of how bad of an idea it is." Parker replies.

"Is it? Then why'd I see you buy one of my turkey balls?"

"I didn't…"

Parker looks down at his tray and finds that a turkey ball that he never picked up has somehow appeared there.

"What the hell?"

"Who do you think has done the best out of us so far?" Curtis asks as Parker continues to try and unravel the mystery on his tray.

"I don't want to talk about that." Ace snaps.

"Not you then, obviously."

Nobody says anything, the exact thing that Curtis wanted to hear.

"Perfect. I still have a shot then. I haven't started selling yet because I'm still working out the final details of my plan. Even so, your reactions tell me that I must not be too far behind."

"My reactions didn't tell you anything." Ace retorts. "I'm just a really humble guy, that's all."

This draws laughter from the entire group.

"Humble. Yeah, and I'm as stupid as you." Parker sarcastically mocks.

"You **wish** you could be as stupid as me."

Parker rolls his eyes and goes back to eating, the turkey ball that was on his tray now on the floor.

"Anyway, I see my target has just entered the room. If you'll excuse me, I have some business to take care of."

Dean exits the lunch line and sits down with his group of friends. Ace crawls underneath the tables to try and avoid being seen by him but he only draws more attention to himself by doing it. By the time Ace makes it to Dean's table, he's already become aware that something's going on around him so he is cautiously observing the space around him. Ace reaches his hand up from underneath the table and tries to pour a bottle of glue into Dean's pudding but gets caught in the act.

"What do you think you're doing? Are you seriously trying to pull the same prank on me you did two days ago?"

"No." Ace innocently answers.

"But yes you are though. I'm seeing you do it."

"Exactly. Last time I did it you didn't catch me until you ate a little bit of it so this is different."

Dean kicks at Ace.

"Get out of here!"

Ace crawls back underneath the tables to his original seat.

"Like I'm not going to try this again tomorrow." Ace comments with a look of indignation. "He can't avoid this."

Chapter 17

Walker, Sheila, and Plat return to their headquarters where Cynthia is waiting for them with two new people.

"Oh good; you're still alive. I thought you would've been dead without someone here to protect you." Plat jokes.

"Will you still think you're so funny after I tell you that I almost did die?"

"Maybe. It depends on what kind of story comes along with it."

"Well I'll tell you. I figured that since I was going to be alone anyway, and that I wouldn't be able to send anyone to respond to the distress signals, I might as well go on a recruiting mission. What have you guys all been asking for?"

"A raise?" Plat guesses.

"You've never asked for a raise." Cynthia responds confused.

"Yeah I know. I just thought that this would be the perfect time to bring up the subject. So now that we're talking about it, can I have a raise?"

"No. Nobody's getting a raise. We all just started here."

"Oh, okay. It doesn't hurt to ask."

Cynthia shakes her head. "Anyway, I was out there walking to my destination when I see an armed robbery in progress. I run in to try and stop it but the robber shoots at me and gets away. He missed my head by only a couple inches. If you had been with me, Plat, you could've shielded me while I used my powers to box him in with stuff."

"So, you're mad because you wanted him to get shot at instead of you?" Sheila wonders.

"It sounds bad when you say it like that. I wanted each of us to be put in the best position to use our talents."

"Yeah, and my talent is being a human shield apparently." A slightly offended Plat comments.

"I'm glad you understand." Cynthia remarks. "I'm just kidding. That's only **one** of your many talents. It's a compliment to say you can take a bullet better than me."

"I'm not so sure it's a compliment. It's more of a fact than anything else. I **am** more durable than you."

"Yes you are. Now can I please tell you guys what it is you've been asking for? These two ladies have been waiting very patiently."

"Is it that they're teleporters?" Ledford asks.

Cynthia frowns. "How'd you know?"

"Because that's something we've asked for. You gave too good of a hint."

"Well, you ruined the big reveal but this is Adrianna and Rebecca Knight. They're teleporters. And if you hadn't noticed they're also twins."

"And they can only teleport to each other." Walker adds.

"Yes!" Cynthia says full of surprise. "Did you read the mind readers' report or something?"

"No, I just figured that that's where this was heading when you said they were twins."

"I read the report." Plat states. "Not a very riveting read at all. Very factual. Kinda boring."

"If I may voice my opinion." Rebecca interrupts. "Even if limited in capability, we both technically have a superpower. So when Cynthia found us and offered us this job we had to say yes."

"That's right." Adrianna continues. "We feel like, as people with superpowers, we have a responsibility to use our powers for good. Under no circumstance whatsoever should someone ever use their superpower to commit a crime. It just isn't right."

"That's a bit overly judgmental don't you think?" Sheila questions. "Some people may have had the best intentions in mind."

The twins both shake their heads in unison.

"No. Crimes are crimes for a reason. They hurt people. When someone uses a superpower it becomes that much more dangerous."

"What if someone commits a crime without a superpower? Is that cool?" Plat asks.

"Absolutely not!" Rebecca answers in shock. "We didn't mean to suggest that at all."

Plat laughs. "You did though. That's your fault."

Cynthia steps in to try and calm the tension.

"Anyway. The plan now is for one twin to be sent out with a group while one stays here. That way she can teleport you all back once the assignment is done."

"Neither of us are much of a fighter so don't expect anything from us out in the field." Adrianna warns. "We were told that you guys would be doing all of the fighting anyway."

"That's right. And if things start to go south, don't expect us to stick around. We'll leave without you, if necessary." Rebecca elaborates. "Our safety comes first."

"I can respect that." Plat says.

"I'd like to discuss this with the current members of S.U.P.E.R.P.O.W.E.R. in private, please." Mathis announces.

Cynthia politely asks for the twins' permission for her and her teammates to excuse themselves.

"Ladies?"

They grant their permission by nodding at the same time again.

"We'll be back soon."

Cynthia leads the group into the conference room that still has no door. They have to go the back corner of the room so Rebecca and Adrianna can't hear them.

"I have some serious doubts about these two." Sheila starts off. "They don't like me. Or Plat for that matter."

"To be fair, they don't know that they don't like you." Cynthia defends. "I didn't tell them that about your pasts. If you want their help, I'd suggest that the topic never comes up."

"Or we could lie." Plat offers. "Because it'll be difficult for me not to talk about my past. It's one of my favorite subjects."

"That works too. Ready to take the vote?" Cynthia asks.

The group all nods.

"Alright then. All in favor of adding the Knights to our team raise your hand."

Cynthia, Walker, and the Platinum Cyborg all raise their hands right away while Sheila is hesitant but eventually goes along with the group.

"Oh alright. I'll allow it."

"We didn't even need to you to allow it." Plat informs. "We already had the majority; your vote meant nothing."

"But we're glad you did." Cynthia shares.

Plat opens the closet of the conference room, pulls a man out of it, and sets him in front of the group.

"While we're voting on things, let's give this guy a vote. I found him using the report last night. He says he's willing to work the night shift."

"Who is this?" Cynthia asks.

"That's a good question." Plat answers. "Go ahead and tell them."

"My name's Keith Weller but you can call me the Lighthouse."

Weller raises his right arm and shoots a beam of light out of his palm. He then does the same with his left arm.

"So your power is that you can project light from your hands?" Ledford asks unimpressed.

"Yep. But it's not good for just seeing in the dark."

Keith turns his lights off then aims his right hand at a chair. He turns the light back on again for only a second but this time instead of just illuminating the chair it instantly incinerates it and burns a hole through the ground underneath it as well. Plat puts his arm around Weller's shoulder and gives him a half hug.

"Pretty cool, right? It turns out that I had actually met this guy once before. My old organization sent me and a couple other guys to scout him but back then he said he could only make light, so we just decided that he was worthless."

"Yeah, but I'm not worthless. I only said that I was because I thought it was better to say that rather than tell them that I just didn't want to work for someone evil. I'd never work for someone evil. I draw the line at neutral. But the Platinum Cyborg tells me that you're trying to do good. That's the best out of the three possible choices."

"That's true. But what I'm trying to figure out is if you were left in the closet overnight."

"He was." Plat is quick to answer." "I had to keep him in there until I found the perfect time to make the big reveal. That's kinda my thing. So are we going to vote him in or what?"

"We need to get Adrianna and Rebecca in here first. They have a vote since they're part of the team now."

Cynthia goes to the other room to retrieve their two newest members, who are unaware of what's happening.

"Can someone explain to us what's going on?" Rebecca asks.

"We tried eavesdropping but there were too many voices coming through the vents." Adrianna informs. "It made things worse, actually."

"Yeah, all we could make out was "we need to get rid of them". That wasn't about us was it?"

"Don't worry about what's going on. Just raise your hand when you're told to." Plat explains. "All in favor of hiring the Lighthouse raise your hand."

The entire group, minus Plat who does it enthusiastically, cautiously raises their hands. The cyborg then gives his newest teammate a pat on the back.

"Congratulations Mr. Weller; you've just been hired to do the work that no one else wants to do."

"It'll be my honor." He says with a bow.

Chapter 18

Ace and his friends are outside of their school after class has been dismissed for the day. Ace pulls his wagon ahead of the group and sighs. Most of the boxes loaded on it are so damaged that their labels can no longer be read, and can no longer even hold their contents any more. Instead loose turkey balls are piled on top of empty, smashed, boxes.

"Well, I'm off to selling again. I've got to add to my lead you know."

"Don't you think you should get some different boxes first?" Rash asks.

"I'd like to but they won't let me return these. I've got to sell all of these first so I'm not on the hook for all of them."

"That's never going to happen." Parker states. "So if you're trying to lose on purpose, then be my guest."

"Suck a ball." Ace retorts as he throws a turkey ball at Parker that hits him in the mouth. "Hey that's a dollar! Pay up!"

Parker snorts as he leaves the group. Ace picks up the turkey ball that is now covered in dirt and gravel and sets it back with the others.

"You didn't see that."

"Nobody was going to buy it anyway!" Grant shouts. "I know that from experience. Thanks to this contest, I'm going to have to do some serious butt kissing to get my Dealr rating back up."

Ace gives Grant a pat on the back.

"Don't worry; if anyone can do a good job kissing butt, it's you. I'm off!"

Ace and his wagon depart from the group leaving Rash, Curtis, and Grant together.

"I think it's time for me to leave without explanation." Curtis announces.

"Good luck, dude." Rash says as he gives Grant a pat on the back as well.

He then walks away shortly behind Curtis.

On his way out of the school yard, Ace makes a stop at Miss Brick's car. He waits there for a half hour until he sees her coming towards him.

"Hey, Miss Brick! I want to say I'm sorry for how things went the other day. You know, for harassing you and stuff."

"That won't be necessary. You're not the only student who's been bothering me for sales."

"I'm not? Damn it! Who else has it been? I'll teach them a lesson for you if you know what I mean."

Ace slowly pounds his fist into his other hand to show his teacher what he meant.

"I don't want you to do that either. You should try listening to the lessons **I** teach **you** in the classroom instead."

"No thanks. I just need to know if you accept my apology or not. I don't apologize to everyone you know. I'm proud of all the mean things that I do to people. The only reason I'm even apologizing to you is because I think you're hot and I don't want this to ruin my chances with you."

With Ace blocking the driver's side door, Miss Brick is forced to get into her car through the passenger's side. She then moves over to the driver's seat and rolls down the window slightly.

"There's nothing for you to be sorry about. **I'm** sorry for running over you. And I'm sorry the school is making you sell a product that no one in their right mind would want. My advice? Just give up. It's not worth the trouble you're putting yourself through."

"No. Not until my friends give up first. But you accept my apology right?"

Miss Brick starts to back away.

"I accept your apology."

"Good! Now do you want to buy some turkey balls? I'm running a special offer. Buy one box, get the second half off."

"No thank you."

Miss Brick rolls up her window all the way and drives out of the parking lot before Ace can make an argument.

Chapter 19

Curtis arrives at the food cart that his parents have set up for him, titled Grayson Sandwiches after his family's last name and the product they sell. His father, Dane, is making the finishing touches by nailing a sign underneath the name that reads: *Don't ask us what our first ingredient is…it's love!*

"I like it." Curtis compliments. "Hopefully people will find that too adorable to actually ask the question. I don't want to answer it. I might have to lie."

"You can't lie, son; that's illegal." Dane informs. "You've just got to be more creative with the words you use. Like instead of saying that it's made with leftover turkey guts you say it's made with a unique blend of turkey products."

"Ahh, I see. That's really good."

"Yep. And that's why I work in marketing. I have a great spot reserved in the business park. If you approve of everything we can get this loaded up and moved there before supper time."

Curtis nods. "It looks good to me."

"It looks good to me too." Rash adds as he approaches his friend.

"Did you follow me here?" A startled Curtis asks.

"Actually I walked a little bit ahead of you and looked back every once in a while to see where you were so that way in wouldn't technically be considered "following"."

"Seriously?"

"No." Rash responds with an offended look on his face. "Of course I followed you here. You were so secretive about your plan. I had to figure out what it was. Very clever. Adding ingredients to the turkey balls before selling them to cover up how disgusting they are. I can't believe I didn't think of that."

"I don't want you copying my idea now."

"I don't want to copy your idea either. I want to take credit for your idea. Make it Grayson Rash Sandwiches and we can split the sales fifty-fifty."

"No! Why would I do that? It's my idea and I don't need your help with it. I needed my mom and dad's help but that's it. You go off and sell your product door-to-door like a good little drone while I'll be in **my** food cart winning this whole thing."

"That's exactly what I'm going to do…not!"

Rash takes a quick picture of Curtis' cart and then runs off.

"Hurry, dad! We need to get going! He's trying to steal my idea."

Dane and Curtis load the cart and all of their other supplies onto the back of a moving truck and speed over to the business park where they unload their cart again and begin preparing their sandwiches. Within minutes the customers start lining up. The customers can order from a menu of a half dozen sandwiches, all made using the Lawson Farms turkey balls in some form.

About an hour into operation, one customer comes forward with a complaint.

"I was just taking a look at the ingredients and I found a discrepancy. Your sign says the first ingredient is love but the ingredients list on my barbeque turkey sandwich says that it may only contain trace amounts of love. Which one is it, sir?"

"Ahh…" Curtis answers, unsure of what to say.

"I'll step in here." Dane announces. "You see, the sign is only a goal. An ideal that we strive for. And while we try to make every sandwich using the maximum amount of love possible, the actual amount of love in each sandwich will vary."

"Oh. So you gave me one that you really didn't care about. That's just great. Also, what's this unique blend of turkey products that's listed as the actual number one ingredient mean?"

"It means exactly what it says."

"Which is? Can you tell me what turkey products exactly?"

"I cannot. We get our meat premade from our supplier. For more information you'd have to contact them directly."

"Or don't." Curtis interrupts. "We're not saying that there's definitely some gobble in there but we also can't rule out the possibility. Our supplier would tell you the same thing."

"And so what if there is?" Curtis' mother, Claudia, asks. "You're hungry. We have food that tastes good. You pay us for that food and then eat it. Let's not make it any more complicated than that."

The customer shrugs. "Yeah, I suppose. It is all turkey right? There's not something else in there that I should be worried about?"

"One-hundred percent turkey." Dane confirms.

"Alright then, I'll take another barbeque turkey sandwich. But make it with more love this time."

"Will do." Dane says with a nod.

The Graysons continue to do good business for the next hour and a half. At that time, a car comes barreling into the park and comes screeching to a stop a few feet away from their cart. Roland and Rash hustle out of the car to set up an old card table that they place a crock pot on top of. Rash attaches a hand drawn sign to the table that reads: *Rash's Fine Meats.*

"Get your turkey ball casserole here!" Roland calls out. "Fresh, hot, turkey ball casserole! Nothing better on a cool October day!"

Curtis steps out from behind his cart to go over and confront his friend.

"Why are you doing this? You're embarrassing yourself."

"No, I'm embarrassing **your**self. Who's going to want your delicious smelling sandwiches when they could have this slop?"

Rash slaps the spoon down into the crock pot, splattering casserole all over himself, Curtis, and the table.

"Don't listen to him, Rash. He's just jealous that he didn't think of this idea." Roland says.

"Yes I did! It was my idea to sell a homemade product using the turkey balls. You just tried to copy me. Unsuccessfully I might add. You didn't even bring any bowls!"

"Yeah, I was hoping I could borrow some from you."

"Hey Roland! Did you even get permission to sell here?" Dane asks.

"What are you? A cop? Mind your own damn business. **Hot casserole here**! **Get your hot casserole!**"

Roland continues his call as Rash watches all the customers go to the Graysons.

"It's not helping, dad. Look at their fancy cart and then compare it to our crummy table."

"I don't want to; it's too depressing." Roland immediately responds.

"That's my point. They put time, money, and effort into this. We didn't bother to use any of those things and yet we expected to have the same amount of success as them."

"There's more to running a successful business than those three things. There's also luck."

"I'm sure they have that too."

"Think again. It seems we have our first customer."

A person appears to be walking towards the Rash's table when they make a hard left turn at the last moment to go the Graysons.

"Got ya!" The person taunts.

"How dare you trick my son like that?"

Roland hustles over to the customer before they can place their order and throws them to the ground. He then stomps on them repeatedly until they're unconscious while Rash and the Graysons just watch it unfold.

"Got ya." Roland taunts back, even though his victim can't hear him.

"I called the police." Dane informs. "So unless you want to go to jail, I'd suggest you get out of here right now."

"That's fine. I don't like the smell around here anyway. It's my own casserole. It's disgusting."

Roland dumps the contents of his crock pot all around the Graysons' cart.

"There. Let's see you sell anything with **that** smell hanging around."

He then folds up his table and loads it back into his car.

"Come on Rash; we'll win this competition some other way."

Roland quickly drives his son out of the business park while the Graysons, as well other bystanders, are forced to cover their noses.

"I never knew that food could smell this bad." Claudia comments. "What did they do?"

"Whatever they did it's getting worse as it sits around." Dane states. "I think we're going to have to call it quits for the day. Roland was right. Nobody's going to want to come near here with that smell."

"That's alright." Curtis says. "We sold ten boxes worth of turkey balls today. All we have to do is do the same thing for the next two thousand four hundred and ninety-nine days and I'll have that A.P.T. The fundraiser only runs through next week though. I don't like my chances."

"That's okay, son. Learning to run a successful business is more valuable than any fundraiser or winning a bet with your friends." Dane explains.

Chapter 20

Grant meets with a large group of his customers in their secret location.

"I'm sure you all know why I've called you here. You've been giving me bad reviews recently. Care to explain yourselves?"

"You deserved it. You're latest product sucked. People have the right to know that."

"It's not my product! It's someone else's. I'm just selling it for them. If you want to leave bad reviews for someone, leave them for Lawson Farms. And for Mann Elementary."

"Just stick to what your good at and we'll start giving you good reviews again. Right guys?"

All the other customers state their agreement.

"About that. I'm actually running a little low on supply at the moment. My supplier was murdered and no one has come to replace him."

"Oh, that's going to hurt your rating for sure. I'm gonna have to leave you a negative review right now."

Grant slaps the phone out of his customer's hand.

"You can't do that."

"Uh-oh. Getting aggressive with a customer. That's definitely a negative right there." A different member of the group declares.

"Quit leaving me bad reviews!"

"He just shouted. That's a negative."

"Stop it!"

"He just shouted again. Reposting the same review."

Grant tries to pull out his own hair in a fit of rage.

"Why are you doing this to me? I've been good to you. To all of you."

"Hey, if you can't deliver the goods, man, people have got to know about it."

"This is the worst thing to ever happen to me!"

Grant starts running around in circles, grunting, and waving his arms.

"I think the reason he's short on supply is because he just got done using it all himself. This guy's crazy. Let's get out of here before he attracts too much attention."

"Don't you dare."

Grant's former customers run off in all different directions. He screams as he chases after them. He's able to catch up to one of them and tackles them to the ground.

"Rate this experience positively or die!"

"Hell no, man. Get off of me."

"Not until you tell all the users of the Dealr app that this was a positive experience for you."

"Alright. Alright. You're going to need to get up a little bit so I can reach my phone first."

Grant shifts his weight enough so the person can move their arm. The former customer is now able to roll out from underneath Grant allowing him to run away.

"**You tricked me!**" Grant shouts as he starts screaming and chasing after the same person again.

The chase ends at the street corner when the person jumps into the bed of a passing truck, gaining them a pace that Grant can't keep up with. However, Grant continues to run and scream throughout the city in the hopes that he'll come across another one of his former customers. He gives up after spending two hours doing this with no success. Thoroughly defeated, he returns to the Mann Hotel in shame.

Chapter 21

Ace takes his wagon to a new neighborhood and goes door-to-door peddling his product. Everyone he comes across takes one look at the condition of the boxes and immediately passes. He doesn't argue. He doesn't try any tricks. At this point he's given up all hope of ever winning the contest…fairly.

He goes up to a guy reading a newspaper on a bench and taps him on the shoulder.

"Pssst. Hey." He whispers. "Do you know where I can find a good counterfeiter?"

"Sure don't." The man answers before getting up and walking away.

Ace stops the next guy he sees to ask him a similar question.

"You look like you've printed some fake bills before. Want to make some for me?"

The man becomes greatly offended. "Excuse me. I do not make fake money. I steal the real stuff."

"Well I don't have any so you're out of luck."

"We'll see about that."

The man knocks Ace over and searches all his pockets, taking the fifteen dollars in ones that he had.

"What do you call **this**?" He asks as he holds the money right next to Ace's face.

"Dollar bills. The same as everybody else. You call it something different I take it."

"I call it you being a liar."

"Hey, now that you've got some money, do you want to buy a box of turkey balls from me?"

"Nope." The man quickly answers as he gets up to walk away.

"Do you want to steal them from me? That'd help a lot too. I could get some new boxes then."

"Don't want to do that either."

The thief tries to walk away but Ace follows right alongside him.

"But what if you bought one box and then just stole the money right back from me? It'd be a win-win for both of us."

"Kid, get away from me."

Ace hops in front of the thief every time he tries to change direction.

"Not until we figure this out. So you say that you like to steal money right? What's the biggest job you've ever done? Enough to buy twenty-five thousand boxes of turkey balls? They're fifteen dollars apiece."

The thief takes a moment to do the math before responding.

"That's three hundred and seventy-five thousand dollars. I've never done anything that big. I'm just a small time street criminal."

"Hey, well now's a good time to jump up to the big leagues. I'll even help you. I could be your lookout. Whatever it takes to get this thing done. Um um yeah!"

Ace starts skipping in a circle around the thief who clearly wants nothing to do with him.

"If I give you your money back will you leave me alone?" He asks.

"Will you steal some money for me afterwards?"

"Nope."

"Then I guess so."

The thief hands Ace back his fifteen dollars and so he stops following him. He does, however, witness the thief pickpocket another person's wallet.

"I don't need that guy." Ace mutters. "I forgot that I'm related to an evil crime lord. I'll just get **him** to help me."

Chapter 22

Ace and Grant arrive back at the Mann Hotel at the same time but Ace is the first to the door.

"Can you hold that open for me?" Grant asks. "My arms are really tired."

"Sure." Ace answers as he lets the door close behind him, right in his brother's face.

Grant struggles more than he should to open the heavy door but manages to do so.

"Sorry. My hand slipped." Ace insincerely explains.

"**I'm not in the mood for your crap**! I just lost all my customers today."

Grant checks his rating on the Dealr app.

"I'm at a negative one. I didn't even think that was possible."

"Anything's possible." Ace taunts. "Like it's even possible for you to be uglier than you are. Hard to believe, but it is possible."

"Does that mean it's possible for you to go a day without making fun of me?"

"Sure. Quit giving me things to make fun of and I will."

"I don't even want to talk to you." Grant concludes. "I want to talk to Cooldaddy about something."

"How interesting. I **also** want to talk to Cooldaddy about something." Ace counters.

"It'll have to wait until I'm done with him."

"Wait. What's that?" Ace yells as he points off at the direction opposite the stairs.

Grant doesn't bother looking and instead runs for the stairs himself. Upset that his trick didn't work, Ace hurries after his brother all the way up several flights of stairs and directly the room that they've been staying in. They bust through the door together and are surprised to see that none off their family members are there and that another family has moved in. The family is surprised to see them as well. Neither party makes a move.

"Well this is weird." Ace comments. "There's a bunch of people we don't know in our room."

Ace takes a step back into the doorway to make an announcement.

"Don't worry everyone; I'm going to fix this. I know you must be lost and confused right now so that's why I'm going to go get security to come up here and kick you out right away. This is the Randar room and you don't belong here."

Each member of the family looks at each other like they have no idea what Ace is talking about.

"No, this is **our** room and **you** don't belong here." The mother responds.

"Look, let's just have security decide who belongs where. P.S., my father is head of security here so things probably won't end up going you're way. Let's go, Grant."

Ace shoves his brother through the doorway then closes the door behind him.

"I don't know about them but I'm definitely lost and confused right now." Grant says.

"You're always lost and confused." Ace snaps. "It's because you do too many drugs. Now move it."

"Yeah I know, but I mean I'm more confused than normal. I'm confused as to why they were in there in the first place."

"The hotel obviously made a mistake. And they damn well better fix it before I get angry."

Ace and Grant march back down to the front desk to try and correct the situation.

"My name is Ace Randar. My father is Dirk Randar, the head of security here. Can you contact him and tell him to have his team kick some unwanted guests out of our room?"

"I'm afraid we can't do that." The new manager, Edgar Hopkins, says as he joins Ace at the front desk. "Your father was terminated when Richard Mann found that he had been hired without his consent. Now I can't just go around ordering civilians to attack other civilians can I?"

"I'm sure you could if you really tried." Ace comments.

"But I shouldn't. Besides, he's not even here anymore. He and the rest of your family got kicked out of the hotel entirely. That's not your room anymore. We gave another family a free upgrade to that room right after they left. They didn't tell you?"

"No. I was at school and then busy doing other stuff that I don't want to talk about."

"And you don't have a phone that they could've contacted you with?" The manager wonders.

"Oh wait yeah. I do."

Ace checks his phone.

"It says right here that they're staying at the Better Stay Motel and some directions are included. Oops."

"It's no big deal. I'll give that family another free upgrade to smooth everything over. You should probably leave right now. You don't want Mr. Mann to see you here."

"That's alright. We don't want to stay at your stupid hotel anyway. We have a house. It's just broken right now. If it wasn't we wouldn't have even had to stay here."

"The best of luck with that." Hopkins says with a bow.

Ace and Grant run out of the Mann Hotel and then start using the directions they were given to find their way to their new temporary home.

Meanwhile, seconds after they leave, Phinn, Ginn and Dinn smash through the windows of the hotel and start firing energy in every direction. Ginn lifts a frightened guest over his head and hurls them across the room. Phinn rolls through the tables as if they were bowling pins. Dinn rips all the art off the walls and throws them at people as they try to run away.

"Give me the Randar family!" Phinn commands. "I know they're here. One of their neighbors told me so."

Hopkins peaks his head over the front desk to respond.

"They're not here. They **were** here but they were forcefully removed just a few hours ago."

"Tell me where they went and I'll spare the rest of your hotel. Don't tell me and my brothers and I will turn this place into the world's fanciest pile of rubble."

"I think one of them said they were going to the Better Stay Motel." The manager informs.

"I don't know where that is!" Phinn screams.

He fires a warning shot energy beam at Hopkins that grazes him on the shoulder, causing him to deform into a pile of dirt. Phinn squeaks in confusion.

"Hey guys; look at what that human just did. They don't normally do that, right?"

"No. I don't think so." Dinn replies. "Let me try it on this one."

Dinn shoots a light energy beam at the clerk who was also hiding behind the front desk. They too crumble into dirt upon impact.

"This one did too. Which is weird. I didn't even hit them hard enough to make them explode. They just fell apart."

"Well it takes three to be a pattern."

Ginn shoots another energy beam at a member of the staff hiding in the corner, producing the same result.

"It's a pattern alright."

"Look at the cool sculpture I made!" Phinn exclaims as he points to the miniature dolphin he created using Hopkins' dirt. "I'll make one of you guys two while you get the directions to the Better Stay Motel off their computer."

"I can't." Ginn informs after trying unsuccessfully to use the keyboard. "The buttons are too small. And I don't have any fingers."

Two guards from the hotel's old security force finally make it down to the lobby but Phinn blasts them immediately causing them to turn into dirt as well.

"There's something wrong with this hotel. It's really starting to creep me out." A shivering Ginn declares. "Is this even worth all the trouble we've been through, Phinn?"

"No. But we're doing it anyway. We'll do what you want to do tomorrow. Right now we've got to find out where the Better Stay Motel is or we'll still be doing **this** tomorrow."

"I found a map of the city's businesses." Dinn informs as he waves it around. "That should help right?"

"Good work, Dinn. How'd you find it?" Phinn asks.

"It was sitting on the desk right in front of you two."

"Okay great. We got what we need now let's get out of here before more dirt people get here."

"And let's destroy your sculptures so no one knows that it was us who destroyed this place." Ginn says as he stomps on Phinn's creations, much to his dismay.

"Hey! I put no effort whatsoever into those!"

"Well that works out because I put no effort into destroying them."

Ginn and Dinn roll towards the exit but Phinn continues to stand still, staring down at the pile of dirt.

"What are you waiting for?" Ginn calls back. "Once we're done beating up your humans we'll stop at an art supply store and get you some clay, alright? I'm sorry."

Phinn doesn't respond.

"You there Phinn?"

Startled, Phinn looks in several directions before finding Ginn.

"Did you say something? I was just daydreaming about fish. I was thinking that we should blow off whatever it was that you said and we should pick up some once we're done beating up the humans.

"Yes, Phinn; whatever you say. Can we go now please?"

Chapter 23

Marlena and Dirk are waiting outside the Better Stay Motel as Ace and Grant arrive.

"Oh good; you got our message. We were worried that you would've gone back to the Mann Hotel. We were just getting ready to check there." Marlena explains.

"And we're not even allowed back there ever again. That just shows how much we care about you." Dirk adds. "And how little we care about their rules."

"Well actually…" Grant begins before he's cut off by an elbow to the ribs from Ace.

"Yeah we both came straight here once we were done selling. No detours of any kind."

"Except when we stopped at the Mann Hotel by accident. That was a pretty big detour."

"No it wasn't Grant; you're just imagining things." Ace scolds.

"I'm not imagining that you're an idiot. That's a real life fact." Grant fires back.

"I know **I'm** imagining that I don't have a step-brother right now." Ace returns.

"Enough you too." Marlena interrupts. "We have some important news to tell you. You know how we promised you that we'd be able to sell twenty-five thousand boxes for you?"

"Yeah."

"Well it looks like we're going to be breaking that promise."

"What? Why?" Ace gasps.

"Because the Best Restaurant Ever already bought boxes from Officer Powell's kid."

"And because Rich Mann just doesn't like me." Dirk explains.

"Officer Powell? You mean like Miranda Powell?" Ace wonders. "My classmate."

"I'm guessing so, yeah." Marlena responds.

"Eh, that's okay. The competition isn't between me and her so it doesn't matter. Parker isn't going to like that very much though."

"Is Cooldaddy here?" Grant asks.

"Everyone's here. Including the former manager of the Mann Hotel who we cost a job. I hope there haven't been any delays in the reconstruction of our house because you are **not** going to find this place to your liking."

"What room?" Grant asks.

"Twelve."

"Do you have a key for me?"

Dirk laughs. "Why would you need a key if there are no locks on the doors?"

"Good point. Outta the way Grant!"

Ace shoves his brother aside and runs into the Better Stay Motel. He's taken aback by the stench as he as he walks through the doorway and starts gagging because of it.

"Geez, did someone die in here? This is the worst thing I've ever smelled!"

Ace pinches his nose and continues on to room twelve while Grant soon catches up to him. Not only does their door not have a lock, there appears to be several bullet holes in it as well. Ace pushes the door open causing it to fall off its hinges.

"Grant did it."

Several scented candles have been lit to mask the smell in the Randars' room. Cooldaddy is lying on the lone bed in the room, a twin, smelling one of the candles.

"Cooldaddy! I never thought I would say this but thank God you're here. I need your help with something. Grant, you don't need to hear this."

Ace tries to shoo away his brother but instead Grant walks further into the room.

"Don't listen to him. I need your help first."

"Cooldaddy doesn't want to help anyone. Except himself. Go away."

"Oh really?" Ace asks. "You'd rather stay in this pit than help your only grandson?"

"Hey!" Grant shouts.

"You're just a step-grandson. I'm the real deal. Help me first."

"Cooldaddy never thought about going outside and doing something to avoid the smell. Maybe that's why everyone is waiting out there instead of here. Cooldaddy just thought they didn't like his choice of candles. Alright, Cooldaddy'll help you. But only so he doesn't have to be in here."

"Sure. Whatever. Let's just get going."

"What about me?" Grant whines.

"Nobody's forcing you to stay in here either." Cooldaddy informs.

"No, aren't you going to help me?"

"Damn it, boy. One thing at a time, okay?"

"But it's important."

"Ooh, that's too bad. If that's the case then it'll just hurt that much more when Cooldaddy doesn't help you right away."

"In the meantime you can help contribute to the smell in here." Ace teases. "You do that everywhere you go already."

Grant pouts in the Randars' room while Cooldaddy and Ace go back outside and to a far enough distance from the rest of the family so they can speak privately.

"You know how to print some counterfeit bills right?" Ace whispers.

"Cooldaddy's done some counterfeiting. Real high quality stuff too. How much are we talking here?" He whispers back.

"Not much. Just three hundred and seventy-five thousand dollars. Enough to buy twenty-five thousand boxes and get the A.P.T. from the fundraiser."

"Sounds easy enough. Cooldaddy's just wondering why you don't just buy the A.P.T. instead. It's cheaper and you wouldn't have to get stuck with all those turkey balls."

"It's not just about the A.P.T. It's about winning the bet I made with my friends. And to give my teachers the money to better educate me with."

"Suit yourself. Cooldaddy can do this for you but it's going to cost you."

"You mean like money? If I had any I wouldn't be asking you for this right now."

"No, he means like a favor. To be called in at a later date."

Ace claps his hands together in excitement.

"Perfect! You'll get me what I want now and then if everything goes right we'll both forget about the favor and I'll never have to pay you back. Um um yeah!"

"Cooldaddy never forgets to call in a favor." He informs in a sinister tone. "For your sake, Cooldaddy just hopes you keep your word."

"Yeah, alright. Just get me that money by the end of next week or **you'll** be sorry."

Cooldaddy chuckles at Ace's comment causing his grandson to shoot him a menacing glare.

"Seriously. You think that people don't want to mess with you? I'm like that too except I'm also crazy."

Cooldaddy laughs even harder.

"You're making Cooldaddy so proud right now."

"**Shut up!** I'm not making you anything."

Ace storms off past the rest of his family on his way back to the motel

"What was that about?" Dirk asks.

"If I wanted you to know I would've included you in the conversation now wouldn't I have?" Ace snaps.

"I suppose. But people don't just tell other people to shut up for no reason."

"Shut up! There. I just did it again."

"That wasn't really for no reason. I was arguing with you. That's one of the most appropriate times to tell someone to shut up. Especially if you can't come up with a sound response to the point your opponent is making."

"Wow, are you trying to bore me to death or what? "

Ace waves off his dad from making any further comment and goes back to the Randars' room to find Grant.

"You're up."

"That was quick. Maybe you can figure out how to fix the T.V. while I'm out there. Every channel is blank."

"That's because it's not plugged in." Ace says as he plugs in the loose power cord.

Grant tries flipping through the channels again now that the T.V. is on.

"Still blank."

"Well maybe it just doesn't like you. Just go out there and tell Cooldaddy your really important thing and I'll fix it."

"No problem."

As Cooldaddy waits for Grant to work his way over to him, the three dolphin brothers leap in from out of nowhere and surround him.

"What the hell?" Cooldaddy says in total surprise.

"I can see them standing in front of the motel." Ginn observes. "We finally found them!"

Cooldaddy stands up to confront the dolphins.

"Hey! If you want to get to Cooldaddy's family you're going to have to go right around him first!"

"You're related to them? Works for me." Phinn says as he grabs Cooldaddy by the beard, spins him around for a while, and then tosses him over the Better Stay Motel.

The sight of Cooldaddy sailing over their heads gets the attention of the other Randars.

"Oh no! They're back!" Dirk shouts. "Everyone hide!"

The dolphins roll over the top of an oblivious Grant on their way to the entrance of the motel. By that time, the other Randars have found hiding spots.

"Ooh! I like hide and seek!" Phinn exclaims. "We've been playing it all day basically."

"Let's just hope that these guys don't have one of those superhero summoning watches." Ginn states.

"Let's just hope you start looking for them." Phinn fires back.

"Found one!" Dinn shouts.

He pulls Old Dirk out of a trash can and shows him off to his brothers.

"I don't remember them having an old guy the last time." A puzzled Phinn declares.

"Let's ask him." Dinn offers. "Are you with the Randars or do you just live in the trash?"

"I just live in the trash." Old Dirk lies, trembling in fear.

"That's disgusting. And I'm touching him. Ew!"

Dinn throws Old Dirk in the same direction that Cooldaddy went.

"Spread out. If you find one of them, beat them up for me." Phinn orders.

Ginn takes the front of the motel. Dinn takes the back. And Phinn takes the inside of the motel itself.

Ginn is the first to find a Randar. Dirk leaps out of a tree and lands on top of his head. Dirk draws his gun and aims for Ginn's eyes. The dolphin whips his head around to try and shake him off but isn't able to.

"Enough of this."

Ginn rolls forward but Dirk jumps off in time to avoid being crushed. He then opens fire at Ginn who retaliates with an energy beam. Both shots miss their mark. Afterwards, Dirk runs back into the trees.

"No. Not again."

As Dirk tries to climb another tree, Ginn jumps up behind him and knocks him down with his tail. He then picks him up off the ground, tumbles forward with him and then launches him into the motel. Dirk ends up rolling to a stop right in front of Phinn.

"Hey! I found one!"

Phinn tosses Dirk back outside next to Ginn who thinks about throwing him one more time but decides against it.

"No. You've had enough."

Dinn continues his search behind the motel. He looks in and under the couple of cars in the parking lot but turns up nothing. He then rips up all the bushes that are lined up underneath the motel's overhang back there but still can't find anyone. Dinn's about to go back around front when out of the corner of his eye he notices Young Dirk standing where a support column should be. He turns back and then stands right in front of Young Dirk and stares directly into his eyes.

"You're hiding so I'm going to assume that you're one of the ones I'm looking for."

"And **I** assume you're going to show me why I was told to hide in the first place?"

"No. I'll let Phinn do that."

Dinn balances on one flipper, spins around once, and then violently smashes Young Dirk through a window of the motel with the back of his tail.

"Just kidding." He laughs.

Dinn then goes to find Cooldaddy and drags both him and Young Dirk up to the front and dumps them next to Dirk. Ginn returns with Grant and adds him to the pile.

"How many of them are there?" Ginn wonders.

Dinn shrugs then lies down on the pile of Randars as if they were a beanbag chair.

"Not enough to make a comfortable chair, that's for sure."

Meanwhile, back inside the Better Stay Motel, Phinn speaks with the clerk at the front desk.

"If it's about the smell you're going to have to be more specific. There are a variety of things making smells, none of which we can do anything about." The clerk is quick to explain.

"No. I wasn't worried about any of that. I want to know if you've seen any Randars recently."

"Sure have. That family is one of the only three guests we have here. How could I forget them?"

"You could have Alzheimer's." Phinn suggests.

"Well I don't. One of the ones you're looking for is standing right behind me disguised as a lamp."

Phinn looks past the clerk and now notices that Marlena had been there the whole time but had been standing completely still while a lampshade covered her head. She continues her ruse even though her secret's been exposed.

"Thank you. And just so you know; if you want something that smells bad, you should try this."

Phinn releases a deep exhale into the face of the clerk, who gags uncontrollably because of it until they fall unconscious while the dolphin laughs.

"See? Now back to business."

Phinn picks up a chair and brings it down over the back of Marlena's head, knocking **her** unconscious as well. He then drags her body to the front door and flings it onto the pile of other Randars.

"I've just got to check the rest of the rooms and then I'll be right back!" He calls out to his brothers.

Phinn rolls back into the motel and knocks down every door until he gets to the Radars' room whose door is already down. He immediately spots Ace just lying on the bed staring at the blank T.V. screen.

"That's not a very good hiding place." The dolphins taunts.

"This isn't a very good place period." Ace retorts. "It smells like crap and who knows what else. There's no locks, no T.V., and the only furniture is this single blood-stained mattress. Obviously I would rather be in my real home but it's been destroyed so I can't."

"And now I have to beat you senseless on top of it. It sucks to be you today."

"Sure does."

Ace finally looks over to see who he's been talking to and is shocked by his discovery.

"Wait! I know you. You're that guy that destroyed my real home. Why are **you** here?"

"To beat you senseless." Phinn flatly answers.

"Oh yeah. You said that already."

"So are we going to do this or what?"

"No thanks. If you wanted to destroy some place you should've destroyed this motel. I hate it."

"No. That would be helping you and I don't want to do that."

"Alright, I'll be seeing you then."

Ace moves to slide off the side of the bed but Phinn launches himself on top of him to keep him in place. The dolphin then starts bouncing up and down on the bed and laughs while Ace is trapped terrified beneath him. Phinn pulls Ace off the bed after he's tired himself out and drags him outside. He then places him with the rest of his family.

Phinn inspects each one of the Randars carefully.

"Looks like we did a good job here, boys. They've all been knocked out but they aren't dead. We hit the sweet spot. Perfect."

"What are you going to do with them now? Just leave them here?" Ginn asks. "Or do you want us to smack them a few more times."

"No. I've got something very special planned for them when they wake up."

Phinn smacks each one of the Randars in the face.

"**Wake up!**"

Every member of the Randar family immediately regains consciousness but stays seated out of fear of further harm.

"What's going on here? What'd we do now?" Dirk asks.

"I came here to teach you a lesson for destroying my home."

"Really? I thought we would have learned that lesson already when you destroyed **our** ome."

"No. I needed to come here and beat you up some more to make sure you fully nderstood the lesson."

"Nope. It was pretty well understood the first time. This was totally unnecessary. In fact probably made the lesson a little cloudier if anything."

"No." Phinn responds with an angry head shake. "This was completely necessary and it leared things up significantly."

"That's not how I see it." Ace informs.

"It doesn't matter whether you think you've learned your lesson or not. All that matters s if **I** think you did or not." Phinn explains.

"What?" A confused Dirk responds.

"I've determined that the lesson hasn't fully sunk in yet. I'm going to have to slap you ach one more time to make sure."

Phinn goes around the circle and gives each Randar one more slap on the cheek.

"Now are you going to destroy the homes of anymore dolphins?"

"I doubt it." Dirk answers. "We never really intended to destroy yours either."

"I see. That's a good enough answer for me." Phinn declares. "What do you think, rothers?"

"It's good enough." Dinn and Ginn both answer.

"Good! We'll be leaving now. Enjoy your putrid hovel and remember: no littering."

The dolphin brothers roll off into the distance as the Randars remained slumped together, nore confused than ever.

"You said they weren't going to know if we threw the broken pieces of our house into the sewer. Obviously they knew." Marlena snaps at Dirk.

"Oops." Dirk responds with a shrug. "My bad on that one. I'll say I'm sorry and then you'll all forgive me right?"

"Nope. Cooldaddy's gonna hold a grudge. But if you wanted to make it up to him by taking him out on a special day where he gets to do whatever he wants, then maybe Cooldaddy will forgive you."

"Nah, your forgiveness isn't **that** important to me."

Dirk gets up and starts walking to his car.

"I'm going to find a different motel. Someone gather up Old Dirk and let's get out of this place."

Chapter 24

Parker sits down with the owner of Akomant Supply, another locally owned convenient store, in the back room to discuss a possible sale.

"So, Mr. Gatlin, I assume it's safe to say that you're human correct?" Parker asks.

The man, who is undoubtedly human, nods.

"You are correct."

"And because of that you are fairly reasonable, am I right?"

"I don't know about that. I think other species can be reasonable as well."

"Other species yes. But not robots."

"Well…I don't know about that either. Robots are usually programmed to be pretty reasonable."

"That's not the point here. I'm asking if **you** are a reasonable man."

"I'd say so." Gatlin answers only somewhat confidently.

"Excellent. Since you're such a reasonable man then you'll be able to clearly see the value of the deal I'm about to offer you. I'm prepared to offer you, for a limited time only, the opportunity to become a proud provider of Lawson Farms turkey balls. A stock of twenty-five thousand boxes can be yours for the special low price of fifteen dollars a box. You're not going to be able to get this deal anywhere else." Parker informs with his fingers crossed underneath the table.

Gatlin folds his hands together and leans back in his chair as if he's seriously considering Parker's proposal.

"You make quite a presentation, Mr. Greiner. My only issue is that there's no room in my budget for a purchase of three hundred and seventy-five thousand dollars. That's more than this store makes in a month. That's more than this store makes in six months."

"Stop, you're being **too** reasonable. Come on, splurge a little. You can take out a loan. I promise you you'll be able to sell these really easily." Parker says with his fingers crossed again, but this time he crossed them on top of the table.

"You just crossed your fingers when you said that." Gatlin points out, putting Parker on the defensive.

"Yeah of course. You know, I'm hoping for you that they'll sell easily. Fingers crossed!"

"Or you were telling me something that you knew to be false."

"What? I would never do that."

For the third time, Parker crosses his fingers as he speaks.

"You **just** did it."

"Damn it."

Parker sits on his hands so he can't make the gesture anymore. However, Gatlin gets out of his chair and opens the door to his office, signaling that it's time for Parker to leave.

"You're a good young salesman, Mr. Greiner, but you have to work on your tells. But, as a show of respect, I'll buy ten boxes from you. If that sells well, then maybe we can continue this conversation later. But until then, please be on your way."

Parker gets up from his own chair and goes to shake Gatlin's hand.

"Thank your sir. Your capacity for reason truly knows no bounds."

Gatlin fills out all the information on the order form and then gives Parker his check who is grinning from ear to ear.

"Thank you again, sir. I have your product right outside. I'll set it at the register on my way out."

"Very good." Gatlin nods.

Parker sprints out the front door, tosses the boxes in the general direction of the register, and then bolts all the way over to the Lightbot Mini-mart. He runs straight into Lightbot GR1's office and drops the order form down right in front of it.

"Look at what your biggest competitor just did."

The lightbot flashes and dings its response then prints out a sheet for Parker to read.

"So what? Am I supposed to be impressed? I take it that you think that just because he did something stupid that I'm supposed to do something stupid as well? It doesn't work that way."

Furious that he didn't get the reaction that he was hoping for, Parker crumples up the paper and throw's it at GR1's head.

"How do you know what's stupid and what isn't? You're just a defective machine who's not even doing what he was made for."

GR1's head glows bright red as it prints another note.

"The only thing that's going to be defective around here is your legs once my friends get done with you."

"Are you threatening me?" Parker asks.

The lightbot shakes its head.

"That's a promise, nerd."

"A promise that you won't keep!"

Parker dashes out the door and straight into the waiting arms of another lightbot. As Parker struggles ineffectively to get free, GR1 relays its message to its friend, then prints a note explaining what it said and holds it up to Parker's face.

"Make his legs into a pretzel. NOT a pretzel stick, though. No, no. Don't do that!"

Parker tries even harder to get free as the lightbots laugh at him. The one holding Parker begins to bend his left leg in the opposite direction of what it's supposed to before stopping suddenly to laugh harder. GR1 then prints out another note for Parker.

"We weren't actually going to do that! I hate pretzels! Break them the normal way."

The second lightbot, LR5, tapes Parker's mouth shut and then punches him in both knee caps, shattering each of them. It and GR1 then walk together out the store as they drop Parker in the parking lot. They then leave a note on top of him that reads:

A promise is a promise, young man. You should ALWAYS keep your promises.

I promise we'll get you home safely. What happens to you after that is up to you.

In the future, learn to make better decisions, okay?

In their own language, GR1 tells LR5 to contact Parker's parents, then returns to its office. LR5 looks down at Parker as it flashes bright green. It shows Parker a note that reads:

This is going to make an awfully funny story for you to tell someday.

Just not to your parents today, understood?

Chapter 25

The Rashes sit around the dinner table in complete silence. Neither Roland nor his son can stand to look at each other so Delilah tries to break the tension.

"I'll give twenty dollars to whichever one of you says something to the other first."

Both Roland and Rash look at each other as if they're considering taking Delilah up on her offer but neither one does.

"Seriously? Fifty dollars then."

Still neither of them budges, frustrating Delilah even more.

"This is getting ridiculous. What even happened out there?"

"Ask your husband." Rash answers.

"Roland, what happened out there?"

"Ask your son." Roland responds.

"How about this? How about you both tell me at the same time and you both came have fifty bucks?"

"Nah, I'm not doing anything with him again." Rash declares. "He'll **try** to help me explain what happened but all he'll end up doing is embarrassing me in front of my friends instead."

Delilah stares across the table at her husband.

"Did you do something to embarrass him, Roland?"

Roland shrugs. "I don't know. It depends on what you consider embarrassing. If you consider creating a product that gets made fun of constantly and gets passed over at every opportunity in favor of his friend's product embarrassing then yes I did. If not, then I didn't do anything wrong."

"I'd consider that embarrassing."

Roland angrily drops his utensils onto his plate.

"Then I guess I embarrassed him, didn't I? I embarrassed myself at the office too and it's probably going to get me fired. Do you want me to talk about that as well?"

Now Delilah is the one who shrugs.

"It'd be nice."

"Well I'm not going to. I don't want to talk about any of this! What's worse is that the Randars probably have sold hundreds of boxes already and they'll only embarrass me even more."

Roland storms off from the dinner table into the living room.

"You suck!" Rash yells out to his father then turns to his mother. "There. I said something to him. Can I have my fifty bucks now?"

Delilah nods and gives the money to her son who then runs off to his room.

"Looks like I'm the one who's going to have to fix this mess… again." She says with a sigh. "Like always."

Delilah leaves her meal, grabs a box of turkey balls and the order form, and heads for the door.

"Where are you going with that?" Roland asks as he points to the box of turkey balls. "I love you and I want you to always be happy. But that trash will bring you nothing but sadness and rage. I can't let you leave the house with that thing. It's pure evil. Rash is just going to have to learn that you can't make stupid bets. If us disappointing him is what it takes to do that then that's what it takes. This'll be a good learning experience for him."

"You want to just give up and let the Randars win? That's something I never expected to hear from you. Maybe this is an experience that **you** can learn from as well."

"Yeah. You're probably right."

Roland gets up to give his wife a hug.

"I shouldn't fight the battles I know I can't win either."

He takes the box of turkey balls from Delilah's hands and tosses it into their fireplace.

"Let's just get rid of that and just enjoy the night together, shall we?"

"You just cost us fifteen dollars. We have to pay for that now." Delilah points out.

Roland's mood takes a dramatic shift as he starts throwing around anything he can get a hold of.

"Damn it! I hate these things!"

Chapter 26

Late at night, the Lighthouse, Keith Weller, sits alone in the old government building. He watches T.V. as he waits for the signal on his watch to go off. Altes soon joins him in the room and moves in to introduce himself.

"You must be Cynthia's newest recruit. I'm Mayor Altes, your boss. It's a pleasure to meet you."

The mayor extends his hand to Weller for a handshake but Cynthia comes up behind him and knocks his arm down by the wrist.

"Liar. He's lying to you Keith. He didn't support the S.U.P.E.R.P.O.W.E.R. program. He doesn't even want you here. By definition it can't be a pleasure to meet someone you never wanted to see."

"Sure it can."

Altes goes for the handshake again but this time Cynthia stops Weller from offering his hand.

"You know, if it was up to him you'd still be working the night shift at that convenient store you used to work at. The one that you said paid you less than minimum wage? What was it? Akomant Supply? That's the one."

Weller looks Altes in the eye while appearing genuinely hurt.

"Is this true Mayor Altes? Why would you want me to work that lousy job when I could be saving people's lives?"

"Yeah Mayor Altes, why is that?" Cynthia reiterates.

"I don't know."

"That's not much of an answer."

"You're right. You deserve better than that. Give me a couple days to work on a better response and I'll get back to you. In the meantime you get after it alright?"

Altes raises his hand for Weller to give him a high-five but he gets left hanging.

"Would you quit trying to touch him?" Cynthia requests. "It's getting weird."

"What's weird is how obsessed you are with your new job, Miss Cromwell." Altes returns. "I didn't think you'd be here this late."

"I didn't either. But no one else volunteered so it had to be me. Which is fine. I already live here and my power will get the Lighthouse to his destination the quickest anyway. Do **you** have a destination that you'd like me to get you to quickly, Altes? Someplace other than here? Like your **own** home perhaps."

"Maybe this is my home too."

"Uh, I hate to interrupt you guys but the signal just went off." Weller informs.

Cynthia quickly checks the coordinates on Weller's watch.

"Got it. Are you sure you're willing to go out alone? I don't want anything bad to happen to you."

Keith nods his affirmation.

"Don't worry about. I wouldn't have signed up for this if I was afraid."

"Alright then. Good luck."

Cynthia sends the Lighthouse out on his assignment then teleports Altes as well.

"Not going to stay alone at night with you so goodbye."

She then turns to watch the television herself. While she waits for Weller's return, the signal on Cynthia's watch begins to blink so she just shuts it off.

"Nothing I can do about that now so off you go."

Ignoring the distress signal does appear to pain her significantly but Cynthia works to distract herself from her thoughts by focusing on the movie she's watching. An hour later she's relieved to see Weller return safely.

"How'd it go?" She asks.

"I've got some good news and I've got some bad news. The good news is that I stopped the home invasion by incinerating the home invader's gun. Along with a piece of the home invader as well. The bad news is that I incinerated a little bit of the home in the process. And by a little bit I mean a lot of bit. They said they're going to sue us now."

"Don't worry about that. I've got a meeting with a guy tomorrow who should be able to help us take care of that. Along with our sleep deprivation."

"I hope that works out."

Chapter 27

The Randars have resigned to the idea of staying in their vehicles for the duration of the repairs on their house and are now parked on the street outside their home. Marlena and Ace are sleeping in her car. The two clones are sleeping in Dirk's car. And Dirk, Grant and Cooldaddy are sleeping in Dirk's Backfire tank.

Grant wakes up Cooldaddy in the middle of the night and whispers to him.

"Is this a bad time?"

"Yes it is." Cooldaddy whispers back as he tries to fall back asleep.

"But you haven't helped me with my problem yet."

"Boy, if you keep preventing Cooldaddy from getting a good night's sleep, you're going to have a lot more problems."

"It'll only take a minute."

"Fine." Cooldaddy sighs. "What's the problem?"

"You're on Dealr right?"

Grant shows Cooldaddy his profile on his phone.

"Of course Cooldaddy's on Dealr. He's not an idiot. That's why he doesn't use a real photo of himself as his profile pic like you do."

Cooldaddy shows Grant his own profile, complete with a picture of Santa Claus.

"People will see that and they'll get the general idea of what Cooldaddy looks like without giving them a clear photo to take to the authorities."

"But none of the authorities are allowed on Dealr. They have a screening process and everything."

"That won't stop some deadbeat you wronged from turning you in to them though." Cooldaddy informs.

Grant is stunned by that revelation.

"I never thought about that before."

"Cooldaddy's advice is that you delete that profile and then come up with a cool street name for your new profile. Something like Coolgrandson, Coolboy, or Coolmale. Just as long as you stay away from Coolfather, Coolgrandfather, Coolpatriarch, or Coolsire. Those already belong to Cooldaddy. Then, after you pick your name, use a stock photo of something that approximates your appearance. For you I'd suggest a rat or a hamster or some other kind of rodent since that's what your face looks the most like."

"Okay, I'm creating a new profile right now. What do you think of Coolgrant for my name?"

Cooldaddy is quick to shake his head at Grant's idea.

"Don't like it. It uses your real name still."

"How about Coolant then? I'll take off the "gr"."

"That's not great but it's better. Now what about the picture?"

"Uploading a picture of a skunk right now."

"Cooldaddy would've just gone with the photo of the hamster but you do what you want."

"Now what?" Grant wonders.

"Now you set your location at a different place than what you had before and disguise your identity once you get there and you'll be set. And don't forget to delete your old one."

"I just did. But I still have the same problem that I came to you about in the first place. I don't have a supplier anymore. That's why my Dealr profile got all of those bad reviews. And that's why I need you to be my new supplier."

"Cooldaddy would be honored. As long as you continue to follow his advice that is."

Grant bows down to his grandfather.

"Of course I will. **I'll do whatever you tell me to do!**"

Dirk kicks Grant from where he's sleeping.

"Shut up, Grant, I'm trying to sleep. You can join Cooldaddy's criminal empire in the morning."

Chapter 28

The Randars wake up the following morning to the sounds of the construction crew working on their house. They all get out of their vehicles while Marlena checks the time.

"It's nine seventeen. You guys are way late for school."

"That sucks." Ace says disinterestedly.

"Get back in the car and forget about breakfast. I'm driving you both to school right away."

"I **had** forgotten about breakfast until you brought it up. Now you're going to have to buy me something on the way there."

"Whatever. Let's just get going."

Ace points a quick finger at Cooldaddy.

"Remember our deal, Cooldaddy. I don't want you backing out on me."

"You don't have to worry about Cooldaddy keeping up his end of the bargain."

"This definitely sounds suspicious." Dirk declares. "I'm guessing you probably shouldn't be doing what you're doing."

"Neither should you." Ace fires back. "**Not** minding your own business? That's definitely something you shouldn't be doing."

Marlena opens the backseat door to her car and pushes Ace inside.

"You're wasting time, Ace. Just get in there."

"We're already going to be over an hour late as it is. What difference does a few more minutes make?"

"That's a few minutes that you won't have to make up later."

Marlena gets into the driver's seat as Grant takes the backseat opposite Ace. She then drops the accelerator to the floor and speeds down the street on the way to the school. Cooldaddy chuckles as he watches them leave.

"Cooldaddy doesn't know why Grant needs to go to school anymore. He's going to come work for Cooldaddy now. You all should. It's better money than not having a job."

"Hey! I have a job." Dirk harshly explains. "It's just that nobody's hired me at the moment."

"I'd work for you if I didn't hate you." Young Dirk adds.

"Why don't you make yourself useful and sell some turkey balls?" Dirk suggests to his younger clone.

"Don't bother. Cooldaddy's got that taken care of. He's going to go make the sale right now."

Cooldaddy shuffles off without another word leaving Dirk to ponder how he could be so confident in his ability to make a sale that he couldn't.

"I don't buy it. But since Cooldaddy says he's got it then why don't you make yourself useful and help the construction crew with their job?"

"I've got a better idea. Why don't I make myself useful and not do anything at all?"

"Well, I don't see how that works but it's better than arguing with you so go do whatever."

"I don't need your permission." The younger clone says as he waves off Dirk.

"I guess you like sleeping in the car then?"

Young Dirk stops walking away and turns right back around towards the Randars' place.

"You got me."

Dirk drags his older clone as he follows behind Young Dirk.

"You're helping too."

Chapter 29

Ace and his friends gather at their favorite lunch table and once again Ace steers the conversation toward himself.

"I woke up late today. Missed the first couple of classes. No big deal though. I've finally got this contest figured out. That's a **huge** deal."

"Sure you do." Rash mutters. "Meanwhile, while you're sleeping in, I'm riding the bus by myself. How do you think that made **me** feel?"

"Good?" Ace guesses.

"Bad."

"Oh. It had to be one of the two. Picked the wrong one. Shoot. So anyway, I'd like to know what happened to Parker. It looks like you broke both your knees."

Parker, who's now in a wheelchair, nods, acknowledging that Ace's assessment is correct.

"I did."

"Care to share how it happened?"

"I fell down a flight of stairs."

"Really? I've done that several times before. I was perfectly fine afterwards all those times."

"So what?" Parker asks defensively. "Just because **you** got lucky and didn't get hurt doesn't mean that it's incapable of happening to someone else. Falling down stairs is still dangerous. I wouldn't tempt fate by doing it anymore then you already have."

"But **I** would though. Tell me the exact way you fell down the stairs so I can recreate the scenario for myself and see if it hurts me in the same way it did you."

"No."

"Why not?"

"Because I don't want to. It was too traumatic of an experience for me. I don't want to have to keep reliving it."

"Okay then." Ace shrugs. "I'll just use my best guess then when I'm trying it at home."

"Speaking about your home." Rash interrupts. "When's that going to get finished anyway?"

"Soon." Ace replies.

"How soon?"

"Sooner than you'd think."

"Oh." Rash says full of surprise. "That's really soon then. This is good news."

Curtis pretends to loudly clear his throat to get Rash's attention.

"We've been sitting here for several minutes now and you've yet to apologize for yesterday."

Rash looks away from his friend.

"I don't know what you're talking about."

"For trying to steal my idea."

Everyone in the group other than Rash and Curtis gasps.

"How could you, Rash?" Ace insincerely asks. "You jerk!"

"I'm not going to apologize because I didn't do anything wrong. You didn't invent the idea of combining products to make a meal and you don't own the business park. I didn't "steal" anything."

Ace gasps again.

"That was your secret idea, Curtis? I'd steal that idea too if I hadn't already come up with a better one."

"**It isn't stealing**!" Rash shouts in frustration. "Tell them Parker."

"I have to agree with Rash on this one. You can't steal a concept that's free to the general public."

"See?" Rash says smugly.

"If that's the case then why don't you share **your** idea with the rest of us, Parker?" Curtis requests.

"No! I don't want the rest of you using my idea."

"Aha!" Curtis exclaims while pointing his finger triumphantly at Parker. "You've just admitted that you don't want someone else stealing your idea."

"Aha nothing. You'll notice that I used the word "using" rather than "stealing". The idea itself is open for anyone smart enough to think of it. Luckily for me, none of you have been smart enough to think of mine yet…as far as I know. Your problem, Curtis, is that you didn't do a good enough job of hiding your own idea while I have."

Curtis shakes his head in disgust.

"Using. Stealing. It's all the same thing. One person per idea. That's what I say."

"Says the person hoarding the good idea." Rash remarks. "I'm alright with you guys using as many of my bad ideas as you'd like."

"Yeah, and what about the "dos" and "don'ts" list?" Ace wonders. "Isn't that encouraging everyone to use the same idea too?"

Curtis nods. "Yeah, and look at how that's worked out for you."

"Hey! I've sold over one hundred boxes to myself because of that list. And because of that jerk, Dean. Which reminds me, I've got some business to go take care of again."

Ace empties a bottle of glue into his own container of pudding.

"This is super glue. I'm not joking around this time."

As Dean is exiting the lunch line, Ace rams into him and knocking his tray onto the ground.

"My bad, dude. Here, let me help you."

Ace secretly switches the puddings before Dean shoves him away.

"I don't want your help. And I don't want your pudding either. It's already been opened, idiot. I know you switched them."

"Fine. I was just trying to make things better between us. Sorry."

Ace holds back a laugh as he returns to his seat.

"I glued mine shut and opened his. He thought it was the other way around but he has mine now."

Ace continues snickering as he watches Dean take a spoonful of the glue then immediately spit it out. That's when Ace erupts into a full laugh causing Dean and his friends to march over his table.

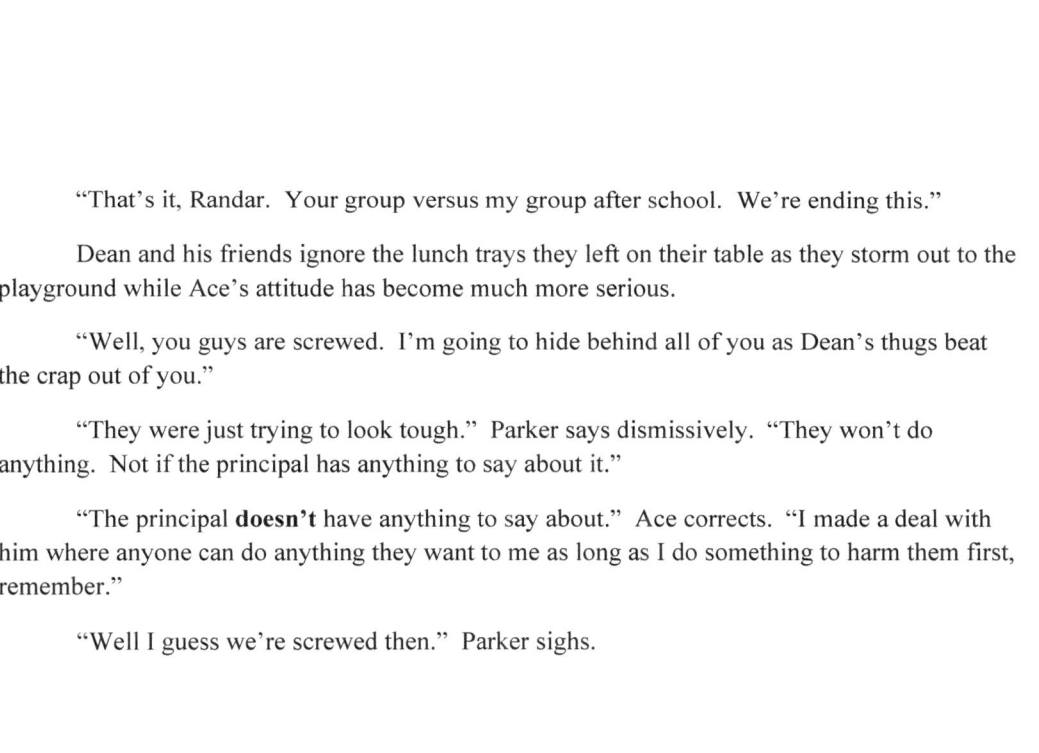

"That's it, Randar. Your group versus my group after school. We're ending this."

Dean and his friends ignore the lunch trays they left on their table as they storm out to the playground while Ace's attitude has become much more serious.

"Well, you guys are screwed. I'm going to hide behind all of you as Dean's thugs beat the crap out of you."

"They were just trying to look tough." Parker says dismissively. "They won't do anything. Not if the principal has anything to say about it."

"The principal **doesn't** have anything to say about." Ace corrects. "I made a deal with him where anyone can do anything they want to me as long as I do something to harm them first, remember."

"Well I guess we're screwed then." Parker sighs.

Chapter 30

Early in the morning, Phinn and his brothers return to Ginn and Lynn's home with Lynn greeting them at the door while holding Dorsal.

"How'd it go guys?" She asks.

"Very well." Phinn responds. "We found them. We beat them up. They learned their lesson. Now they're never going to bother us or any other dolphin ever again. But man am I tired though. I could really use a nap."

Phinn immediately crams his way into Dorsal's crib. For a few seconds it holds his weight but it comes crashing down right after that.

"Ow!"

Lynn stares down at Phinn disdainfully.

"What did you think you were doing? That was **Dorsal's** crib."

"It was? I thought you left that out for me. I guess that would explain why I didn't fit in it."

"How **is** Dorsal? And how are you?" Ginn asks his wife. "You're not still mad are you?"

"No. We're both fine. I'm getting used to the name. It's not like your name is that great either."

Ginn squeaks in surprise.

"You don't like my name?"

Lynn quickly changes the subject.

"Dorsal said his first word while you were gone. He said "tuba". Which is weird. I never said the word to him; he must've just stumbled upon those sounds by accident."

"Cool! I hope you were able to record it."

"I was. I'm wearing a camera at all times so I don't miss any of his firsts."

"Dinn…" Dorsal says out of nowhere.

All the dolphins are surprised as they stare at Dorsal.

"He said his first name!" Ginn exclaims. "And it was my brother's for some reason."

"That **is** his middle name as well." Dinn reminds. "Or maybe he just likes me the most. can't blame him."

"Er" Dorsal continues.

All of the dolphins now share the same confused look on their faces.

"Did he just make a random noise or was he was he actually trying to say "dinner" this whole time?" Lynn wonders.

"I was trying to say dinner." Dorsal explains.

The group has now gone from confusion to complete shock.

"He just said his first complete sentence!"

"I know. And I'm hungry. I want dinner." Dorsal declares.

"I'm stunned right now." Lynn announces. "If you could say whole sentences already hen why did you make your first word "tuba.""?"

"I didn't mean to. I just made those sounds by accident as I was testing my voice. What was really trying to say was "tuna". As in I'm hungry so go get me some tuna."

"This is amazing. You must be some kind of genius if you know how to speak before anyone teaching you." Lynn gushes.

"And I'm also really cute too."

Lynn hugs her son tightly.

"Yes you are!"

"Enough about Dorsal already." Phinn whines. "Let's start talking about me again. Where am I going to stay if not in that crib? Do you have a spare bedroom for me?"

"We did have a spare bedroom but that's going to become Dorsal's room." Ginn informs.

"Okay. I'll just room with him. You wouldn't mind sharing a space with your Uncle Phinn would you Dorsal?"

"Well, actually…"

"It's settled then! Dorsal just said it's okay for me to stay with him."

"I didn't say anything." Dorsal argues. "You cut me off before I could finish my thought."

"That's just because we know each other so well I can finish your sentences for you. All the more reason why we should share a room."

"There's a room you can have in the basement." Lynn explains. "You and Dinn."

Phinn tries to stay positive about his given living arrangements even though the news is difficult for him to bear.

"Oh. Alright then. I guess it's better than living in the sewer. It's not as good as living on the ground floor with your nephew though."

"But that was never an option for you." Lynn tells him.

"You don't hear me complaining." Dinn says. "That's because I'll be doing it all later once we settle into our room."

Dorsal waves goodbye to his uncles.

"That's what you get for naming me Dorsal. Now you have to live in the cold, dark basement while I get a warm, well-lit bedroom."

Phinn steps toward Dorsal menacingly.

"That's pretty smug coming from someone I could punt like a football."

Dorsal cowers underneath Lynn's flipper.

"Mommy, help! He's threatening me!"

Lynn slaps Phinn across the side of the face.

"Phinn! How could you? He's just an infant."

"I know. That's what made it so easy." He laughs.

Lynn slaps Phinn again with Ginn following up with a slap of his own.

"That wasn't funny." Lynn scolds. "Do you want the basement or not?"

"I don't know if "want" is the proper term here. It'd be more appropriate to ask if I'll accept the basement or not."

Lynn slaps him for the third time, followed by Ginn, and then Dinn.

"I don't need the visit from the grammar police. Either take the basement or don't but don't threaten my child."

Phinn rubs the sore spot on his face.

"Okay. I'll take the basement. But I just want you to know that he started it."

As Phinn heads to the basement with Dinn, he turns to look back at Dorsal one last time and has his glance returned by the infant sticking his tongue out at him. Phinn considers saying something to the child but feeling the pain in his face makes him decide against it. Instead he makes a comment to Dinn.

"Where did that kid get his attitude from? It certainly wasn't from me."

Chapter 31

The members of S.U.P.E.R.P.O.W.E.R. are all together in the conference room, waiting for Cynthia to arrive and start the meeting.

"Hello everybody." She says as she walks through the doorway. "Just a couple things today. I'm going on a recruiting mission today so I won't be here to send anyone on any assignments. That means you're going to split up into two groups and go and patrol. Spread the good news about S.U.P.E.R.P.O.W.E.R. to the people of Akomant."

"Can I make up some fake stuff as long as it's positive?" Plat asks.

"No. Just tell them how we plan on making the city a safer place. Walker, Sheila, and Rebecca will be group one. Plat, Adrianna, and Keith will be group two. Ladies, you know what to do if either one of your groups gets in trouble."

The twins both nod.

"Run away as fast as we can to save ourselves. We know."

"No. You're supposed to teleport your group to the other one to help out."

"That's **not** what we agreed on." Rebecca states. "We told you that we were going to avoid the fighting at all costs and you were okay with it."

"That's what you said." Adrianna reiterates. "You can't say it's okay one minute and then not okay the other."

"We're going to leave it up to a vote." Cynthia declares. "Who thinks the twins should try and save the rest of you if they can?"

Plat, Mathis, Ledford, and Weller all vote yes.

"Who thinks they should leave you for dead at the first sign of danger?"

The twins are the only ones to vote yes for that option.

"I can't believe this!" Adrianna exclaims. "We have no means of defending ourselves. Why would you make us do this?"

"Because your teammates will defend you, that's why."

"I don't like it. This isn't what we signed up for." Rebecca grumbles. "We could be trapping ourselves in who knows what kind of problem."

"That's why you've got to communicate with each other. That's what your watches are for. Now go out there and earn your paychecks."

Plat readies the rocket in his right arm.

"With pleasure. I'm going to blow up the first criminal I see. That'll send this city a message; next time, don't be the first person I see."

"You'll use the appropriate amount of force." Cynthia corrects.

"I'll use the **in**appropriate amount of force on the first criminal I see."

"Whatever. Just make sure you don't harm any civilians."

"Oh I'll make sure I don't harm any civilians alright." Plat says as he readies his other rocket leading to some confusion for Cynthia.

"Wait, were you being sarcastic about that?"

"No, I wasn't being sarcastic at all." Plat answers in a somewhat sarcastic tone.

"But that was…nevermind. You know better. I hope. The other team's left already. You need to get going."

Plat stops to whisper to Cynthia on his way out.

"I like to joke but know that I truly would never intentionally hurt an innocent person. That time in my life is behind me. Please don't fire me."

"Not intentionally but by accident though, right?"

"Oh, I'd hurt people accidentally all day long."

"Please don't."

"I don't have any control over that. That's why it's an accident."

"Just go."

Group two exits the conference room just before Altes enters it.

"We need to have a serious talk about your behavior, Miss Cromwell. You can't just teleport me whenever you feel like it. Yesterday, I ended up stuck in my chimney because of you."

"I'd love to discuss this with you further but I can't right now. I have some things that I need to do. Why don't you come back at another time okay?"

Cynthia taps Altes on the shoulder and sends him away again.

"Or not at all, preferably."

She then leaves on her own assignment while group one begins their patrol. Within the first couple of minutes out on the street, Sheila and Walker foil an auto theft attempt while Rebecca stands by and watches.

"You guys are amazing. How long have you two been doing this?" She asks Mathis and Ledford. "You're obviously very comfortable with it. You must have plenty of experience."

Walker shakes his head. "No. Just a few days. We were hired not much sooner than you."

"Really? But you must have been fighting crime on your own before then right? That's how you got so good at it."

"Something like that." Sheila answers while trying to avoid the subject.

"My sister and I would have fought crime too if our teleportation power wasn't so awful. There's not much we can do with it. Except make a two way trip half as long. Or be together when the criminal beats us down."

"Yeah, not everyone can have a power as good as Fr…"

Ledford stops before he can finish his sentence then pulls Sheila aside and whispers.

"We need to come up with a different superhero name for you quick. If I would've used your supervillain name like I almost did, Rebecca would have flipped out and probably left the group."

"I never really liked that name anyway. It's just what people gave to me. It doesn't bother me to switch it."

"So what do you want to be called instead? Hurry up and pick something before she gets suspicious."

"How about Show Stopper?"

"I already said the "fr" sound. It's got to start with that or she won't believe it."

"Well that severely limits our options doesn't it? Aw, that would've been an even better name. Speed Limit. I want it. Make it work."

"Sorry about that." Walker says to Rebecca who was waiting patiently by reading a magazine she found on a bench. "I had to tell her what my social security number was. We made a bet yesterday as to whose numbers added up to be higher but I didn't know mine right off hand. But since now that I just remembered them, I thought it would be a good time to tell her mine. Then she told me hers. Then we added them up and it turns out that it's a tie. Who knew?"

"Oh. I thought you would've been discussing who it was that had that awesome superpower who started to tell me about."

Ledford pretends to cough.

"Right. As I was saying: not everyone can have a power as good as freezing time like Speed Limit over there."

Sheila tries to wave off the compliment.

"Oh please. I don't freeze time. I just slow things down extremely far. That's why they call me Speed Limit and nothing else."

"The name suits you." Rebecca says with a smile. "My sister and I also came up with some superhero names for ourselves. I'm Teleport and she's Ation."

"I'm sorry; did you just say she's Asian?" Ledford skeptically asks.

"No, **Ation** as in "teleportation." I get the first part because I was born first. She gets stuck with the weird part because she was born second."

"I'm sure she's got to be happy about that." Mathis comments.

"Hey, if she wanted the better part of the name she should have come out first, simple as that."

"Why don't we keep moving?" Walker calmly suggests. "I'm sure someone's out there waiting for us to help them tie their shoe or something."

"That I can do." Rebecca says proudly.

During the course of the rest of their patrol, group one stops three muggers, an arsonist, seven vandals, and one petty thief. They then sit down in an alley to reflect on their day.

"We actually helped more people today by **not** using these watches than if we would've waited for someone to contact us with them." Ledford declares.

"But that's because only two dozen people have watches though, isn't it?" Rebecca asks. "I'm sure a lot more people would ask for help if they could."

"I suppose that's true. It's a good thing they don't, though, or we'd be sent running around the city all day."

Rebecca is appalled by Ledford's comment.

"You mean it's a bad thing that they don't. It's our duty as superheroes to save everyone at all times."

Sheila frowns. "**Our** duty?"

"**Your** duty." Rebecca corrects. "It's my duty to get you back to base quickly. And to provide encouragement as you do it. Go you!"

"Right." Mathis says with a roll of her eyes.

"Don't give me that look. If my teleportation power was better I wouldn't need you either."

At that moment a man in a cloak steps out of the shadows of the alley and into the middle of group one.

"I thought I heard people talking out here. You must be the new recruits I was sent here to collect."

Walker steps up to answer for the group.

"We're new recruits. Who are you?"

"I'm the one who was sent to collect you. But first you must answer this question. Where does the wise owl go at midnight?"

Ledford looks to Sheila and Rebecca who look back at him with the same look of confusion that he has.

"Ahh, I don't know. Out hunting I guess."

Startled, the man in the cloak takes a step back.

"Oh, I must have made some sort of mistake. I'll be on my way. But first, one last question for you. Care to join me for a bubble bath?"

Walker is now more confused and disturbed than ever.

"Pardon me?"

The man blasts Ledford with a stream of bubbles from out of his hand, immediately sending him into a deep sleep and causing him to drop right to the ground.

Sheila shouts into her watch. "The Whip is down! We need back-up here immediately!"

"I'm out of here."

Rebecca teleports to her sister before the reinforcements have any chance to arrive.

"Looks like it's just you and me then."

Mathis runs toward the visitor who tries to hit her with the bubbles as well but she catches them in her slowing field and is easily able to roll underneath them unharmed. As soon as the man realizes this, he turns and runs with Sheila following closely behind him.

Just as Sheila is about to get close enough to slow him, the man propels himself into the air using a couple of more highly pressurized streams of bubbles. He then lands on top of a nearby building. The two stare each other down for a moment before Sheila decides to go check on Walker rather than pursue her target.

Back in the alley, Mathis checks Ledford's pulse and discovers that he's still alive, then reports on the situation to the other members of S.U.P.E.R.P.O.W.E.R.

"We just encountered a supervillain. He took down the Whip and escaped. Teleport fled immediately."

"*I warned you that I was going to do that.*"

"*And I wouldn't have gone there to help.*" Adrianna informs.

"*What would have happened if you both had tried to teleport to each other at the exact same time?*" Plat asks.

"*We'd have ended up where the other one used to be. It's happened before.*"

"*That's boring. I was hoping you'd open a rift in space or something.*"

"*What do you mean that the Whip was taken down?*" Cynthia asks. "*He's not dead, is he?*"

"Asleep, I think. He has a pulse and he's still breathing."

"*That's a relief. Return to headquarters and await further instructions. All of you.*"

Chapter 32

Cynthia meets with her latest potential recruit at his dining table in his home.

"Thank you for agreeing to meet with me Mr. Marsh. I'm called the Vanisher. I work for the city as a superhero and I would like you to as well. You can't tell because of my mask but I didn't get any sleep last night and it's taking its toll on me. It's my understanding that your hypnosis powers can give people the same effects as a full night's sleep in just one hour. Is this true?"

"That it is. That's how I run my business. I charge one hundred and fifty dollars per session and that person never has to sleep again."

"Hmm, a hundred and fifty dollars per person. It'd definitely be cheaper if he came to work for us instead." Cynthia thinks out loud. "So, would you like to quit your business and come work with me as a city employed superhero? You'll make one hundred and twenty-five thousand a year."

Marsh appears greatly offended by Cynthia's offer.

"That's it? I already make over a million a year. I serve over thirty clients a day."

"Yes, and I'm asking you if you want to stop doing that and start making less as a superhero."

"No thank you."

"Why not?"

"Because I already make more money now. I thought I made that clear."

"Not everything is about the money. Sometimes you have make sacrifices in order to make the world a better place."

"True. Too bad this isn't one of those times, though."

Cynthia sighs in exasperation.

"Well then can I at least get a discount for grouping four people together at once?"

"No."

"Why not?"

"Because you're still going to use my services without a discount, that's why."

"You don't know that. I could walk out that door right now if you don't give me the price I want."

"Go right ahead. I don't need your business. **You** sought me out. Not the other way around."

"Yep. You're right. But are you sure there isn't anything short of making a veiled threat towards you that I can say to convince you to come work with me instead?"

"I'm sure."

Both Cynthia and Marsh get out of their chairs to shake hands.

"Well then I think our business is concluded here. I'll be needing your services every day at nine A.M. for four people at the old government building and the city will be paying you your usual rate."

"It's a deal."

"Good. Though wouldn't it be a shame if you needed **our** services at some point?" Cynthia says ominously. "Let's both hope that doesn't happen."

Chapter 33

At the end of the school day, Ace stretches as he and his friends wait on the playground for their fight with Dean and his group.

"You guys ready to get your asses kicked?"

"No." Curtis quickly replies. "Are you?"

"Almost. Just got to get my ass loosened up a little bit more and then it should be ready for some punishment."

Ace takes one more big stretch.

"There. That should do it."

"What's Dean waiting for anyway?" Curtis wonders. "I want to hurry up and get this over with. I have that bet of ours that I need to go out and continue to win. Every minute I'm here is a minute I'm not using to sell turkey balls."

Dean and his friends Ken, Hector, and Devin all walk out of the school together and stand in a line a few feet across from Ace and his group of friends.

"I see that you showed up. That's too bad. I was hoping I'd get to call you a coward."

"You could definitely still do that." Parker informs. "You just wouldn't have any evidence to support your claim and thus you could be called a liar."

"Yeah, that's why I'm not going to do that." Dean snaps. "Instead my guys and I are going to beat you down all over this playground."

"Oh yeah? Well there's five of us and only four of you." Ace taunts.

"Hey, look at that. He learned to count. When'd that happen?" Dean taunts right back.

"A while ago. I just forget sometimes that's all. You're not going to be able to count the number of times I punch you in the face. Cause it's going to be a lot."

"We'll see. Get 'em!" Dean orders.

Devin takes Curtis, Hector takes Grant, and Ken takes Rash with Dean charging Ace at the end. Parker wheels around to get a few dozen feet behind Dean's group as no one matched up with him.

Ace's group is outmatched in size in every matchup with the exception being Curtis' and shows early. Hector catches a punch from Grant and then immediately tosses him to the ground. Ken restrains Rash with a choke hold. Dean takes a punch from Ace in order to deliver a harder one of his own that knocks Ace down. Curtis keeps his arms up to block the incoming blows from Devin.

Just as Ken is about to choke out Rash, Parker barrels his chair into his back, forcing Ken to break his hold and to be brought to his knees. Rash takes this opportunity to punch Ken in the crotch as hard as he can. As soon as he falls to the ground, Parker runs over him multiple times to ensure he stays down.

Meanwhile, Hector kicks Grant repeatedly as he lies helplessly on the pavement.

"Come on. I'm down already. You can stop kicking me any time now."

He kicks Grant one more time in the face, knocking him unconscious. Hector then moves on to help Devin who has been on the losing end of a boxing match with Curtis. Rash and Parker move to join that fight as well.

Ace has recovered from his hit and rolls to avoid another from Dean. He then gets up and tackles his adversary to the ground. Dean flip's Ace over so now **he's** on the top of the struggle. He punches Ace in the face a couple of times before he gets his fist batted to the side and then thumbed in the eye. Ace slides out from underneath Dean and then tackles him down again. They then proceed to roll around the playground in a battle to be on top.

Curtis delivers the knockout punch to Devin's jaw just before Hector delivers a knockout blow of his own to the back of Curtis's head. Hector's victory is short lived as Rash comes up behind him and chops him down at the knees. Parker finishes the job by running his motorized chair through him at its full speed of thirty-five miles per hour. Parker and Rash then move on to help Ace.

Dean sees them coming and hurls a rock at Parker's head, knocking him out cold. His chair keeps running until it forces him into the side of a car in the parking lot. The distraction does, however, allow Ace to come running up behind Dean and kick him in the back. He tumbles forward into a right hand from Rash. He then falls backwards into a jab from Ace. Rash lands one last blow to the side of Dean's head that sends him to the ground. Once there, Ace gets on top of him and punches him in the face twenty times. He then gets up and he and Rash congratulate each other with a high-five.

"There. This just goes to show you that you should never try to out-bully a bully. How many times did I end up hitting him anyway? I lost count."

Rash shrugs. "I don't know. I wasn't counting at all. Let's just say fifteen times."

"Sounds good to me. How's everyone else doing?"

"They're all down."

"Good. Now I can get out of here quick without them bitching about how this is my fault. Is the bus still here?"

"It should be. The fight didn't take that long."

Dillon Gross bursts out onto the playground and immediately notices all the bodies lying around.

"Oh no! Am I too late for the fight? Damn, I wanted to grind Randar's face into dust."

Ace becomes aware of his nemesis' presence on the playground and hurries off to where his bus should be, motioning for Rash to follow him

"What's **he** doing out here? Hurry up, Rash; let's go before we find out already!"

Chapter 34

In the early evening, the members of S.U.P.E.R.P.O.W.E.R. wait in the conference room as Plat arrives while carrying Sheila and Walker under each of his arms. He sets Sheila down on her feet and the still asleep Walker gently onto a chair.

"I'm back." He announces.

"We can see that." Cynthia informs.

"I couldn't tell if you did or not because no one said "hello Plat" or "welcome back Plat" or "we missed you". None of that. Not at all what I was expecting."

"Hello Plat!" Keith says overeagerly.

"Too late. My feelings are already hurt."

"When are they not?" Cynthia wonders. "Whatever. It doesn't matter right now."

"Oh, I know my feelings don't matter to any of you." Plat complains.

"Shh. There are more important things to discuss right now. Like what happened to Walker."

"You know some might say that emotional health is just as important as physical health." The Platinum Cyborg argues.

"He got hit by some mysterious man's bubbles and then just fell asleep." Sheila explains. "I requested backup but we all know why **that** never showed up. Because of it, the suspect got away."

Rebecca shrugs. "He should've been more careful around strangers that hide in alleys. Especially strangers that ask weird questions. I did what any smart person would do in that situation. Run."

"What kind of questions exactly?" An intrigued Plat asks.

"He wanted to know where the wise owl goes at midnight. And if Walker wanted to take a bubble bath with him. It was **so** strange."

Plat pounds his fist through the conference room table.

"Damn it! I knew it! I know that guy. He's a member of the Rawrik Crime Organization. That first question is the password we used to use for admitting new recruits. You should have brought me there. We could have captured him and he could have led us to his boss, the head of the largest crime organization in the city. Taking them down would've been a big deal for me! I mean us. As a team. It would've looked good for a team of crime fighting superheroes to take out the most dangerous group of supervillains."

"No way." Adrianna says with a shake of her head. "If you want to go after them that's up to you. But I've heard some terrible stories about them. They're way too dangerous for me and my sister."

"Yeah, it's a good thing I left when I did." Rebecca adds. "If you start messing around in their business. You disappear. Or so they say."

"Do you know when Walker's going to wake up then?" Mathis asks Plat.

"He'll be up in twenty-four hours. It's no big deal."

"Are you sure?"

"One hundred percent."

"How can you be so certain?" Adrianna asks.

"Because I used to work with the guy." Plat answers proudly.

"**What**?" Rebecca and Adrianna both exclaim.

"Oh yeah. He and I used to do some awful stuff together back in the day. Horrible stuff. The kind of stuff that you're afraid of."

"You mean, you were a part of the Rawrik Crime Organization?"

"Yep."

"No he wasn't." Cynthia quickly interrupts. "He's just trying to scare you and you're letting him do it. He got that information from my father's mind reader report."

"No I didn't. I read the report. It wasn't it there. I got that information from my memory of the time I spent with that guy over many years."

"Shut up, Plat. You're not being funny anymore." Cynthia angrily orders.

"Yes I am. I've maintained the same amount of humor throughout the course of this discussion."

"Just give us a straight answer." Rebecca pleads. "Were you a part of that organization?"

Plat answers "yes" while Cynthia answers "no" at the same time.

"Hey, Plat. Why don't you go see if your friend Pine will build us some more watches?"

"I've already asked him. He said he will whenever he damn well feels like it."

"Why don't you ask him again? Right now."

"I guess I could see if he's felt like it between yesterday and today. You know, there's a funny story about my friend Pine. He **also** used to work for the Rawrik Crime Organization."

Cynthia teleports the Platinum Cyborg to Pine's house before trying to uncomfortably laugh off his antics.

"What a jokester that guy. Always trying to lighten the mood with his tall tales. What I'm saying is that he's a filthy liar and you should never believe a word that comes out of his mouth."

"So Walker's **not** going to be alright then?" A fearful Sheila asks.

"No, you can still believe that part. Just not any of the other stuff."

"Well can we see that report you were talking about so we can find out for ourselves?" Adrianna asks.

"No. It's for my eyes only."

"Then how'd **he** get a hold of it?"

"I don't know. I must've accidentally left it in the bathroom stall once I was done in there."

"So you're saying Plat uses the women's bathroom?"

"Hey, I don't know if he used it or not. All I'm saying is that I saw him go in there after me. What he did in there is his own business."

"What about the business **you** went out to take care of?" Weller asks. "Did you get the guy to help us with our problem?"

"That's still to be determined but it's not looking good."

"Aww man, I don't wanna get sued for trying to help someone. It's not nice."

"You know what else isn't nice?" Altes asks as he storms into the room. "Constantly teleporting someone against their will. I've informed the city council of your actions and they told me to tell you that they'd like to have a word with you."

Seeing Altes immediately reminds Sheila of the time he tricked her into thinking she was being set free, only to be led to her death instead. She quickly turns her back to him so he can't see her face then activates her slowing field as an added level of protection.

Weller walks up to the mayor assuming he wants him as well. This also serves to further block his line of sight to Mathis.

"You want us to come too then?" Keith asks just to be sure.

"No, just her. The rest of you can go home."

"But Rebecca, Adrianna, and I were going to work the night shift." He objects.

"That's okay. I'm sure that the people of Akomant will be fine without you for one night."

"I'm not so sure about that. If that were the case, none of us would even need to be here."

"That's right. You **don't** need to be here. I'm quite sure that tonight is a night you can miss."

"Based on what exactly?" Adrianna wonders.

"Based on me not wanting you to be here. I'm your boss; now get going!"

"Hey! You can't talk to them like that." Cynthia defends. "They can stay. They have important work to do."

Altes and Cynthia stare each other down for a moment.

"We'll let the council decide."

"Of course. But only if it's a decision I agree with." Cynthia admits.

"It won't be." Altes states confidently.

The two walk together to the council room where its members are waiting for them.

"Thank you two for coming. This shouldn't take long." Councilman May explains.

Altes takes his seat at the head of the council while Cynthia continues to stand before them.

"I was told that Mr. Altes made a complaint to you all about the work I was doing. You're just going to dismiss that because he's a liar and can't be trusted right?"

"Unfortunately no." Councilman Webster answers. "We have security footage that clearly shows you using your powers to teleport Mayor Altes. He says that he never asked you to do it. So we're faced with a situation here where you forced someone to go someplace against their will. That's kidnapping. That's illegal."

"So is being a thief. He stole that job. It's annoying how many times I have to tell you that without you accepting it as the truth."

"There's no concrete evidence against him for that. There is against you, Miss Cromwell. Mayor Altes said he won't press charges if you agree to step down from your position in S.U.P.E.R.P.O.W.E.R. and no longer seek employment by the city of Akomant."

"He'd like that, wouldn't he? He just doesn't want me around because he knows that I know the truth."

"The truth that you're going insane, just like your father?" Altes sneers.

"No, the truth that he fired you."

"Miss Cromwell, I can assure that those words were never said to me."

"Liar."

"That's enough of that." Councilman May interrupts. "She's obviously not going to step down so are you going to press charges then, Mr. Altes?"

Altes pauses for a moment as he makes his decision.

"No, I don't think I will. Doing so would only make her believe there is some validity to her claims. Which there isn't. I deserve this job. And I'm willing to continue to work with her. I just wished she could say the same about me."

"It's settled then." Councilman May announces. "You're free to go Miss Cromwell. But I'd suggest that you stop using your powers against our mayor without his permission, okay?"

"No." Cynthia defiantly responds. "If anything I'm going to start doing it more now. Not just when he's being intrusive, but also when he's minding his own business too."

"I'd strongly advise against that." Councilman Ross adds. "We really like the work you've been doing. Don't do anything to ruin that."

"That was never my intent."

Cynthia calmly walks back to the conference room where she is immediately approached by Sheila. She whispers so the other members of S.UP.E.R.P.O.W.E.R. can't hear their conversation.

"He's the one."

"What?"

"The guy who just wanted to see you. He's the one that lied to me and had me killed. If it were up to me, I'd say you've been well within your rights to do whatever it is you've been doing to him."

"I couldn't agree more. He's a horrible person. But he's the mayor now. The council tolerated my actions this time but it seems I won't be able to get rid of him without causing more trouble for us."

"You don't like him either? I thought you told me you had a good relationship with the mayor?"

"I did. When my dad was the mayor. But then my dad had a talk with Mr. Altes there and he went nuts. Kind of like…"

"Kind of like what?" Mathis asks.

"Kind of like what happened to you." Cynthia thinks to herself before trying to ease Sheila's curiosity. "Like another encounter I had with Altes years ago."

"Oh. Years? I'm sorry you've had to know him for that long."

"Me too. Let's just keep this conversation a secret between the two of us for now okay? We don't want our boss to know that we hate him right?"

"Yeah. You're right. I'll keep it a secret. I was going to keep **myself** a secret from him."

"Good. You **should** stay as far away from Altes as you can. Keep the others away from him too. But don't let anyone know that you're keeping them away from him. It'll ruin the secret."

"Got it. Will do."

Chapter 35

In the morning, just as Ace is about to leave for school, Cooldaddy drops a duffle bag full of counterfeit money in front of him.

"Cooldaddy's got the stuff you requested. You just make sure you don't tell anyone where you got it from."

Ace opens the bag slightly to check out its contents for himself and is pleased with what he sees.

"Aw yeah! This is perfect. I can't wait to see my friends' faces when they see me turn all this in. They'll be devastated. And I'll be cruising around in my new A.P.T. with two hundred of their dollars in my pocket. Um um um um um yeah!"

"Just a piece of advice. When you turn in the order form you're going to want to put down a fake name. Do **not** use your own. Cooldaddy knows the value of using fake names. Trust him when he says that this step is completely necessary. Then, if anyone asks, have a story prepared for how you know this person and why they ordered so many turkey balls."

"I've got it. I'll have a rich crazy uncle who eats and drinks nothing but questionable turkey products."

"Lastly, if anyone starts to poke holes in your story or discovers, however unlikely, that those bills are fake, don't mention Cooldaddy's name. You're going down on your own for this if it comes to it, got it?"

"Got it."

"Good. Cooldaddy's got a duffle bag he has to give to Grant next that you don't need to know about."

"Whoa, hold on there. Grant's getting a bag too? You're not helping **him** win the bet too are you?"

"Cooldaddy can't discuss the business he has with your brother with you."

"You're not discussing it. You're just answering a simple yes or no question."

"Cooldaddy can't answer a simple yes or no question about his business with your brother either."

"Can you show me what's in the bag at least?"

"No! Cooldaddy can't do anything involving Grant, you, and what's in the bag, other than keeping what's in the bag away from you before he gives it to Grant. Understood?"

Ace tries to slap the bag out of Cooldaddy's hands but he pulls it out of the way just in time.

"Don't do that either."

"You'd better not be double dealing here, old man."

Before Cooldaddy can respond, Grant joins in on the conversation.

"Hey, is that the stuff you promised me?"

"It sure is. Best stuff that money can buy."

"Good. I need the best to restore my reputation."

Ace looks back and forth between Grant and Cooldaddy, trying to figure out what they could possibly be talking about.

"I'm confused. How can a bag of money be the best stuff that money can buy? I'm really struggling with that concept. You can't **buy** money. Unless it's a bag full of those commemorative coins or something."

"It's a bag full of none of your business." Grant retorts. "If you're so interested in what's in my bag, why don't you tell me what's in your bag first? Then I'll tell you what's in mine."

"Mine's full of air. There. I told you. Now tell me what's in yours."

Grant sets his bag behind him, crosses his arms, and then squints at Ace.

"I don't believe you. If it really is just air in there then I should be able to squish that down really easily."

"Go ahead. Give it a try it."

Ace holds out his bag so Grant can try and compress it. He can't as it's packed full with money.

"Wow, Grant, that's so embarrassing. You're so weak that you can't even deflate an empty bag? Man, it sucks to be you."

"That's because there's something other than air in it!" Grant shouts. "I'm going to go wait for the bus."

Grant runs off behind their house while Ace goes to meet up with Rash. They then rejoin each other at the bus stop. When they arrive at school, Ace immediately hurries to the auditorium to turn in his order form. The person directly ahead of him in line is his friend Curtis.

"What's with the bag, Ace?"

"Oh, nothing special. I just made a huge sale, that's all."

Ace unzips the duffle bag and shows Curtis that it's full of twenty and fifty dollar bills.

"Oh really? Who in their right mind would buy that many turkey balls?"

Curtis rips Ace's order form out of his hands and is immediately surprised by what he sees.

"You? How did **you** get that much money? I thought you were poor?"

Ace begins to panic as he now realizes that he must have accidentally put his own name down rather than a fake name as he was instructed. Trying not to seem too suspicious, he decides to just go with it.

"I just pulled it out of my ass like a magician."

"What magician do you know that pulls things out of his ass?" Curtis questions.

"Ah, The Amazing Obscuro. That's who. It's his final act."

"Never heard of him."

Ace sighs. "Yeah, not many people have."

"Well I might as well not even turn this thing in if that's how much you sold to yourself. I thought I was going to be able to with this thing with two hundred boxes sold."

"You thought wrong." Ace smugly responds.

"Clearly."

"Hey, at least you get that foam football. Fifty more and you can get that t-shirt. You can even use that t-shirt as a rag to wipe down my A.P.T. for me, loser."

"You know at the very least you could be a gracious winner. We get it. You spent three hundred and seventy-five thousand dollars to win two hundred. Good for you."

"It **is** good for me. But it wasn't just for the two hundred dollars. It was also for the right to **brag** about winning the two hundred dollars. And for the A.P.T. And so my teachers can start teaching me good. Everyone's a winner here. Except you four. You're all the losers in this story."

"Just hold on there. The week's not over yet. I'm just assuming you're going to win but we don't know if Parker, Grant, or Rash are going to do anything to surpass you. So I'd just hold back on the name calling for a few more days if I were you."

"They won't. I'm going to win. And you all are just going to have to accept that."

Curtis places his order for one hundred more boxes then gets out of the line with his product. He watches as Ace drops his duffle bag in front of the Lawson Farms representative.

"That'll be twenty-five thousand boxes, please."

"Really?"

Ace tenses up as the representative looks through the bag of money, inspecting a couple bills in detail.

"Huh. And it's all for you?"

"That's what the order form says."

"Huh. It probably would've been cheaper to just buy your own A.P.T."

"Geez, what's the deal with everyone saying that?" Ace lashes out. "It's not just about the A.P.T. okay?"

"You could've bought the A.P.T. and made a hundred thousand dollar donation to your school and you still would have spent less than this. I probably shouldn't be saying this but only ten percent of the sales are going to your school. Your school's only getting thirty-seven thousand five hundred of this. Another fifteen percent is going to cover costs and the rest is going to line the pockets of the Lawson family. They really didn't want you to make it to twenty-five thousand. Twenty-four thousand nine hundred and ninety-nine would've been ideal for them. That way they wouldn't have to buy you the A.P.T."

"Tough. I won it fair and square as far as you know."

"Not too tough though. They get it directly from the manufacturer at the wholesale price. It only costs them twenty grand."

"That's not really fair but it doesn't matter. I have to buy as many boxes from them as I can so I can win the bet I made with my friends."

Ace kicks the bag of money closer to the representative.

"So there's my money and my order form. Take them both and give me my boxes so we can make this official already."

"Unfortunately we don't have that many boxes on hand at the moment. We'll deliver them to your house by the end of the day instead, alright?"

"Ugh, fine." Ace groans. "Only problem is that my house is not exactly what you'd call "finished"."

"That's okay. All we need is an address. And you filled that out on your order form. We should have your order dropped off before you get home from school."

"Can't wait." Ace comments sarcastically.

Chapter 36

In the old government building, Plat enters the conference room to report to Cynthia.

"I forced Pine to decide on building some more watches over the weekend. I just finished distributing them this morning."

"That's great." Cynthia responds with disinterest.

She doesn't even bother to look at the Platinum Cyborg. She just continues to stare at the wall deep in thought.

"Hm. I thought you would've been more excited to hear that. Is something wrong?"

"Several things, actually."

"I said I was sorry for messing with the twins the other day. What more do you want? You want me to stop being honest with them? I'll try. I can't do much more than that."

Cynthia shakes her head. "It's not that. Well, actually it is kind of that. They have good reason to be afraid of the Rawrik Crime Organization. Even my dad left them alone. I'm just wondering if we're getting in over our heads here. I don't want to get you guys killed over my own personal mission."

"Should I be honest here, or do you want me to lie to you to make you feel better?"

"I don't know. How convincing of a liar are you?"

"Somewhat."

"Not good enough. You probably should just tell me the truth. Are these guys as dangerous as I've heard?"

"Well let me put it this way: yes. Almost everyone in the organization has a superpower. Those who don't usually get some enhancements done like me. But I wouldn't say that we're in over our heads. We've got a good team coming along here. Get a few more of the right people and we should be able to challenge them."

"About that. I was told that there's only room in the budget for five more members. Or, if we each take a pay cut of twenty-five thousand, six more."

"Well you know that's not going to happen." Plat quickly dismisses. "But, you could also look at it from this angle. If we each take a pay **increase** of twenty-five thousand, then there'd only be enough money for **four** more members."

"And obviously **that's** not going to happen." Cynthia returns.

"Why not?"

"Because it's stupid. We need as many people on the team as we can get."

"I could ask Pine if he'd like to join."

"He basically already has. He charges us for everything he does for us."

"Oh, that reminds me."

Plat takes a folded sheet of paper out of a compartment on his hip and hands it to Cynthia.

"That's the latest bill. The price of the watches has doubled."

"Can you give it to Altes for me? I don't want to go anywhere near him."

"What makes you think that I do?"

"No one **wants** to but someone has to. If it's me, I'll end up teleporting him someplace that'll get me into even more trouble."

"Fine. How about I just fax it to him?"

The Platinum Cyborg drops open a panel on his chest and inserts Pine's bill into the slot that was revealed.

"Although…" Cynthia continues. "If I teleport him someplace he can't come back from, it could **solve** my problem instead. There would be no witnesses to hold me accountable for his disappearance if I do it outside of this building."

After completing his fax, Plat hands the paper back to Cynthia.

"Man, you really don't like this guy do you? And I thought that I held a grudge. What did this guy do to make you hate him so much?"

"It's just who he is. He's always so shifty and sneaky. Not to mention creepy. He was always screwing things up for my dad and embarrassing him because of it. Then, of course, when he was about to get fired my dad had to go crazy and I had to give him a time out. But now that my dad's not here, no one will believe me that Altes shouldn't be here anymore. I don't like it. I don't like how things played out. It's very suspicious."

"Thanks for telling me that. I'm going to go tell him what you said."

"**What**?"

Plat pretends to turn to leave but then stops and starts laughing.

"Got you!"

"Don't ever do that again." Cynthia orders with a combination of anger and relief.

Plat appears to be offended.

"Obviously I'm not going to do it again. Who plays the same joke on someone twice? An amateur, that's who. And I'm not an amateur."

"Just help me decide who on this list should be our final five members will you?"

Chapter 37

Outside the Randars' place, Dirk, Marlena, and the two clones sit on lawn chairs and watch the construction crew work as they near the completion of the home repairs.

"It's about time!" Young Dirk shouts to them.

"About time for what?" One of them stops to ask.

"For you to be done. You **are** almost done, aren't you?"

"Yeah, we've just got to install a few appliances and it'll be done."

"Good. So what are you wasting time talking to me for? Hurry up and get that done already."

The crew member grunts his displeasure with Young Dirk's attitude but gets right back to work.

"That was rude." Old Dirk comments.

"You're telling me. That guy should show more respect to his employer." Young Dirk replies.

"I wasn't talking about him. I was talking about you."

"No way! I was just politely explaining to him that he should have been a little quicker with this job, that's all. I was totally within my rights to do so."

"I'm sure they were doing the best they could."

"Oh really? And how do you know that? You're not their supervisor."

"Yes I am." Old Dirk replies with complete seriousness.

"Then I should blame **you** for them taking so long?"

"But they didn't even take that long. It's only been a week. That's pretty darn fast."

"Hey! If it's not done as fast as I want it to be then it's too long okay?"

"Oh, I can't deal with this anymore."

Old Dirk gets up out of his chair and starts pacing back and forth near the curb. A dump truck carrying all twenty-five thousand boxes of turkey balls that Ace ordered parks in the street alongside him. Curious as to why he's there, Old Dirk questions the driver through the passenger side window.

"Ah, excuse me. I believe you've made some sort of mistake. We didn't order this."

He turns his head back to the other Randars.

"Right?"

"No, I wasn't able to make my sale." Marlena answers.

"Me neither." Dirk adds.

"And I didn't even bother trying." Young Dirk offers.

Old Dirk turn his head back to face the driver.

"See? No one here ordered this many boxes."

The driver looks utterly confused.

"This is fifteen twenty-four Kestrel Street isn't it?"

"Yes…"

"Well then here you go."

The driver pulls slightly away from the curb and unloads all of his cargo on top of Old Dirk.

"Oh God help! **Help!**" He screams as he gets buried underneath the piles of boxes.

His task complete, the driver then speeds away from the Randars' place, leaving a mound of boxes on their boulevard. The other Randars are now more confused than the driver was.

"What the hell just happened?" Dirk wonders.

Marlena looks at one of the boxes to make sure that it is what she thinks it is.

"Ace or Grant didn't make a huge sale did they? They must've but how? They don't know anyone with that kind of money."

"What are we going to do with all of these is the bigger question." Dirk declares. "We can't eat 'em unless you want to puke your guts out."

Young Dirk opens a box and starts throwing each individual ball at the Rashes' house.

"Come on guys, help me out here."

"We'll just have to wait until Ace and Grant get back to see if this is really their doing first." Marlena informs. "Then make a decision from there."

"You're right." Dirk agrees.

Young Dirk returns to the pile to select his next box of ammo. He finds the fingertips of Old Dirk's outstretched hand underneath it and is barely able to make out his muffled plea.

"Help me. Please."

"Oops, sorry."

He sets the box back down right where he found it, completely concealing Old Dirk once more. He then takes another box from a different part of the pile and proceeds to throw its contents at the Rashes' house as well. He repeats this process while Dirk and Marlena continue to monitor the work on their house until he sees Ace, Rash, and Grant turn onto the street together. By this time, The Rashes' front lawn is completely covered in turkey balls with raw meat splattered across their walls and windows. Young Dirk doesn't wash or wipe off his hand before offering a high-five to Ace as arrives home.

"Up top."

Ace immediately avoids all contact.

"Nope."

"What about you?" He asks Grant.

Grant's too busy checking his Dealr rating on his phone to know Young Dirk is even here.

"Excellent. Back up to five stars."

"Hey! That's good news! High-five!"

Grant hears Young Dirk that time and gives him the high-five without even thinking about it, then goes right back on his phone.

"Whoa! What's going on here?" Rash wonders, as he finally notices the pile of boxes.

Ace notices the pile now too and is quite impressed.

"Wow, looks like they weren't kidding. They really did get them here fast. Nice."

"So this **was** you." Marlena states. "How'd you sell that many boxes? You couldn't even sell the first one hundred you got."

"I'm not allowed to say."

"Cooldaddy."

Ace shrugs. "I'm not allowed to say."

"Well, the only reason you wouldn't be allowed to say is if it was something illegal."

"You cheated?" Rash asks in shock.

"Hey! There's nothing in the rules against cheating!" Ace fires back. "And actually, we never came up with any rules. That's why you could get away with trying to steal Curtis' idea. And that's why I could get an unlimited amount of money from an unknown source."

"Cooldaddy." Marlena says again in an attempt to get Ace to confess.

"Unknown source. That's all I can say. I don't even know where it came from."

"So you're saying that one day you just magically woke up with over three hundred thousand dollars?"

"Hey, some people are just born lucky. I'm not one of them. I had to work for my luck. Luckily for me it showed up in time for me to win the bet."

"You haven't won the bet yet." Rash defends. "I could still steal your idea and beat you with it."

"Good luck. You're not going to get it out of me."

"Tell me how you got all that money!"

Rash reaches his arms out as if he's going to strangle Ace but is stopped by Marlena's shout.

"Wait! Before you start fighting can you tell us what you planned on doing with all of these boxes of turkey balls? We can't just leave them sitting here."

"Why not?"

"Because it's an eyesore. And also because Old Dirk's buried under there. I think we should just dump them down the family table. Young Dirk wants to vandalize Rash's house with them. So you need to tell us if you had anything special planned for them before we just go ahead and do what we want to do."

"He can vandalize Rash's house with them or you can toss them. Either one's fine. I don't care. I don't even want them."

"Hey!" Rash yells, clearly upset with Ace's response.

"What? They have to go somewhere. It might as well be on your lawn instead of ours."

Rash charges Ace again.

"That's it. You're going to tell me how you got that money so I can buy turkey balls to vandalize **your** house with."

Ace and Rash roll around on the ground with their hands on each other's throats. Dirk, Young Dirk, and Marlena start throwing the full boxes of turkey ball over at the Rashes' house until another member of the construction crew comes out to speak with them.

"I'm sorry for interrupting whatever it is you're doing but I need to tell you that the work's complete. You can go back into your house anytime you want now."

"**First one in**!" Grant shouts before he bolts straight through the opened front door.

Still locked in the struggle with his friend, Ace releases his grip and gouges Rash in both eyes instead, causing him to release his grip as well.

"That had to end at some point."

He then steps on top of Rash on his way into the house.

"Thanks for the time efficient work." Marlena says to the construction worker. "Do you want to help me carry some of these boxes onto our family table?"

"That's a lot of boxes. I'll get the rest of the guys to help too."

With the help of the construction crew, the Randars move all of the boxes to either the Rashes' lawn or the sewer and then rescue Old Dirk from underneath them.

"Oh it was horrible. I thought I was dead for sure. But now it's over and I never have to see another box of turkey balls again."

"Think fast!" Young Dirk yells as he throws a box of turkey balls at Old Dirk's head, knocking him unconscious and drawing dirty looks from both Dirk and Marlena.

"What? He didn't see it." Young Dirk defends.

"Well now you're the one who has to carry him inside." Dirk informs.

"It was worth it."

"And you Rash. You've got a huge mess to clean up. You'd better get over there and help your parents right away."

"My dad's not going to be happy about this." Rash warns. "He's going to come back at you so hard."

"He can try. We'll be ready."

Chapter 38

The members of S.U.P.E.R.P.O.W.E.R. once again meet in the conference room, this time to vote on whether to allow the group of people Cynthia has brought in for consideration to become the final few members of their team. Walker is the last to arrive and he takes a seat next to Sheila.

"I'm so glad that you're alive." She whispers to him as he sits down. "I'd have felt **so** bad if you would've died back there."

"Me too." Ledford chuckles quietly.

"Nope." Plat, seated on the other side of Sheila, interrupts. "You wouldn't have felt anything anymore."

"Thank you, Plat." Walker responds sarcastically.

Cynthia walks into the room and stands next to the group of six people she invited.

"It's good to see you're okay." She says with nod towards Ledford.

"Thank you." He says with a nod back. "It's good to **be** okay."

"Now that we're all here we can get started. I was hoping to fill out the rest of our team today so I've brought before you the six best candidates I could find. First I'd like to know by a show of hands how many of you are willing to take a pay cut of twenty-five thousand dollars or more?"

Cynthia glances over her audience for a second and sees that no one raised their hand.

"Nobody? Oh well. It was worth a shot. The thing is, we only have room in the budget to hire five people. It would've been six if you all would have been willing to take a pay cut but you weren't so I'm going to have to ask you to leave."

She points to the person to her immediate right, a man who calls himself Ostrich Boy.

"You. You're number six."

"Who? Me?" Ostrich Boy asks as he points to himself.

"Yep. You. Please leave. Don't make this more uncomfortable than it already is."

"Why am I number six?"

"Don't ask questions. Just go. Please."

"Whatever."

The crowd does everything they can to avoid eye contact with the man as he exits the room.

"Now that that's out of the way we can vote on the remaining five people. First we have Corina. Please step forward and demonstrate your power and then maybe tell us a little about yourself."

Corina steps forward as instructed.

"This'll be the same for the rest of you as well." Cynthia quickly adds before sitting down with the rest of her current teammates. "Okay, please continue."

"My name's Corina Price. I'm twenty-six. I've lived in Akomant my whole life and I'm currently a waitress. I'd consider myself to a really kind and caring person who can be a little adventurous at times. I want this job because I think it'd be more fun and more lucrative than waiting tables all day. This is my power."

She forms a small ball of energy in her hand and then lets it float up in to the air until it reaches the ceiling where it sits doing nothing other than giving off a faint glow.

"Is that it?" Plat asks.

Corina shakes her head. "Just wait for it."

A few seconds later the ball explodes, blowing a huge hole in the ceiling.

"Oops. Sorry. I didn't think I put that much into it. You asked for a demonstration though right?"

"Don't worry. It's alright. You did just fine." Cynthia reassures. "Next."

Corina steps back and the next person in line steps up, a humanoid alien with blue skin and a crescent shaped head.

"I'm Cozzig. I would be about thirty of your Earth years. I moved to this planet a few months ago and am struggling to find work. I'm a bit of a comedian which didn't fit in well on my home planet of Caklit. Everyone always takes everything so seriously there. Perhaps because it's a constant struggle for survival with all the viscous beasts there. Or they just don't like me. Either way my superpower is that I become indestructible when I change form."

Cozzig squeals loudly as his body compresses itself into a foot and a half tall ball.

"Well, we'll need to see if he's really indestructible." Plat declares. "Hey Corina, hit him with your strongest energy ball."

"Not a good idea." She's quick to reject. "That'd kill everyone in this room. Possibly the city. I've never tested my full power."

"Fine. I'll do it myself then."

The Platinum Cyborg grabs Cozzig and throws him up through the hole in the ceiling. He then fires two rockets into him as he hangs high up in the sky, exploding on impact. Through the cloud of smoke, Cozzig plummets back down to the ground. He lands with a thud in front of everyone waiting anxiously in the conference room. There he lies motionless as the group wonders if he's alright.

"Oops. I think I just killed him."

Still in ball form, Cozzig begins bouncing up and down in excitement.

"See? Didn't hurt a bit."

"That's a relief."

He begins to change back into humanoid form when Plat forces him back down into his sphere form.

"Wait, what are you doing? I want to get out of here."

The cyborg starts dribbling him like a basketball, from hand to hand and between his legs.

"Cool. I don't care what everyone else thinks. I think we should keep this guy around. He's too much fun."

Plat hurls Cozzig into the wall causing him to deflect back into his hand. Cozzig tries to change form again but Plat keeps his hands on top of him, preventing him from doing so.

"Please get your hands off of me. I don't want to stay like this forever. I'm going to have to use the bathroom at some point and there's no way for me to do it like this. I'll end up just…leaking."

"Ew, gross."

Plat bounces him one last time off the ground as the other members of S.U.P.E.R.P.O.W.E.R. retake their seats. While in the air, Cozzig springs back into humanoid form.

"Tah-dah!"

"Thank you, Cozzig." Cynthia compliments. "And thank you Plat for being such an eager assistant. You can stop with that now unless someone asks you to. Next."

"Hello. I'm Erik Jenkins. I'm twenty-eight. I'm a human. I'm not exciting or interesting in anyway. The store that I worked at recently went out of business. That's why I need this job. Here's my power."

Erik stands in place and blows fog out of his mouth until the entire room is shrouded, except the area underneath Sheila's slowing field, so no one can see anything, including the bow he takes after his demonstration.

"That's it."

The fog slowly filters out through the hole in the ceiling and the meeting doesn't resume until it's all gone.

"Thank you, Erik."

Erik steps back and the next person in line steps up.

"I'm Felicia Carson. I'm twenty-one and I'm a college student. I enjoy spending time doing anything outdoors. I don't need this job whatsoever as I have my career already planned out but I'm here anyway. I have the power to speed up objects over whatever distance I choose."

She walks over to the wall to the right of the audience members and waves her hand forward. A three foot wide line on the floor starts glowing up until a few inches away from the other wall. She steps onto the line and is sped over to the other side of the room with the floor ceasing to glow behind her after she crosses over it.

"In case you were wondering, the object comes to a complete stop at the end of the line of light. You won't go crashing through a wall or another person unless you want me to make you do that."

"Very good, Felicia; I'll keep that in mind." Cynthia says with a nod. "And finally we have Miles Denson."

Miles takes the stage for the final introduction.

"You already know my name. What you might not know is that I'm twenty-four and I work for my family business, Denson Electric. When I'm not doing that I'm watching T.V., going to the movies, or playing video games. I have the power to open wormholes. Only problem is that I can't close them. Once they're there, they're there forever. Unless you find someone else that has the power to close them 'cause I can't do it."

"Can we see a demonstration?" Plat asks.

"I don't think I should. You'd be permanently stuck with a wormhole in this room."

"Just do it you coward." The cyborg angrily orders. "Otherwise how will we know if you really have that power?"

"Alright, a small one."

"You don't need to do that." Cynthia interjects. "We believe you. You should never do something that you think will put your teammates in harm's way...Plat."

"He said just a small one. That's not going to hurt anyone. Besides, I really want to see it."

"Me too." Sheila adds. "If this really works we won't have to rely on you or Teleportation so much. You could get some actual rest."

"I already know it works. We don't need a demonstration." Cynthia argues.

"Everyone else had to." The Platinum Cyborg responds. "It wouldn't be fair if this guy got a free pass."

"None of the other people's powers can permanently change the space around them. That's the difference here."

Plat starts pounding his fists lightly on the table and chanting.

"Show us. Show us. Show us. Show us. Show us."

Cynthia rubs her forehead in frustration.

"Alright already. If you quit acting like a child I'll have him show you."

"Yay!" The cyborg cheers with a clap of his hands.

"I'll put it in the corner."

Miles walks over to the top right corner and taps his finger in the air once. He then pushes a pencil into the exact same spot he tapped his finger. It disappears and then reappears in the air momentarily in the bottom right corner of the conference room before falling to the ground.

"There you go. That's there forever now. I have to trace my finger around where I want the wormhole to open so you don't need to worry about me opening one on you without you knowing about it."

"Do a bigger one." Plat requests.

"No."

"Please?"

"No."

"Why not?"

"Because we've already established that it's too dangerous."

"Well I guess you're not going to get **my** vote then."

Cynthia gets back up and stands in front of the group of prospective recruits.

"Anyway. That's a good way to transition into me telling you that it's time to vote. Just remember that these people are the ones I thought were the best available so if you don't vote for them then we'll have to find someone who's less than best."

"You mean someone bad?" Keith wonders.

"I don't want to answer that. Let's vote! Who wants to vote for Corina Price?"

Everyone in the group raises their hand.

"That's what I thought. How about Cozzig?"

It's a unanimous vote for Cozzig to join the team as well.

"Excellent. How about Erik?"

Only Rebecca, Adrianna, and Cynthia raise their hands for him much to his surprise.

"What the hell guys? Come on. I need this job."

"We only voted for you because we wanted someone on the team with a lamer power than ours." Rebecca explains.

"My power's not lame."

"Sure it is." Plat agrees. "It's just fog. That's not going to do anything. Can we get that first guy that we sent away back instead?"

"No." Cynthia immediately answers. "His power really **was** lame. Technically he had super speed but he said he could only run about as fast as an ostrich. He also said that he runs **like** an ostrich. He seemed to be a little too obsessed with ostriches for my liking. He even had a long neck come to think of it."

"So then why'd you even bring him here?" Walker asks. "Did you just want to embarrass him or something?"

"No, I wanted you to know how thin the talent pool was…by embarrassing him. That being said I think we should take another vote on Erik."

"Wait! Let me demonstrate some more of my power. I can release other gases as well, not just water vapor. Watch me put helium in this balloon."

Jenkins pulls a balloon out of his pocket, fills it with his breath, ties it, and then releases it into the air. It floats straight up to the ceiling.

"See?"

"Lame." Plat comments.

"No it isn't. What do you want me to do? Would you rather have me exhale some radon instead?"

"Couldn't hurt." Plat says with a shrug.

"Actually, that's **exactly** what it could do." Cynthia objects. "What you've done is good enough for now. Now please vote for this guy so we can move on. Show of hands; who wants him in?"

Again Cynthia, Rebecca, and Adrianna are the only ones to raise their hands. Cynthia looks around at the group for answers.

"He just threatened to kill us." Keith explains. "If he wouldn't have done that I would have voted for him."

"Same here." Sheila adds.

"I'm sorry Mr. Jenkins, it's a no."

"You guys suck."

Erik storms off to the exit. Once there, he takes a deep breath and acts like he's going to blow it at the group but stops himself before he does.

"Just kidding. I disagree with your decision but I'm willing to accept it. Thanks for the opportunity at least."

With those parting words, Erik leaves allowing the members of S.U.P.E.R.P.O.W.E.R. to proceed with the final two votes.

"Up next it's Felicia."

Everyone is in agreement that Felicia should join the team.

"And finally we have Miles."

Everyone except the Platinum Cyborg raises their hands once it's time to vote.

"Told you I wouldn't vote for you."

"Well we don't need it." Cynthia declares. "It's six to one. I would now like to formally welcome our new teammates, Corina, Cozzig, Felicia, and Miles! Congratulations to all of you."

They all bow and personally thank each person that voted them in.

"Now, I said I wouldn't but, should I call Ostrich Boy back for a vote or do guys just want to leave that fifth slot open just in case someone better comes along?"

"You can call him back so we can vote him down." Plat suggests. "It was funny when we did it to that other guy."

"I'm not going to call him back if no one's going to seriously consider him."

"You probably shouldn't call him back then."

"Then this is our team. I hope you guys are ready for the hard work that comes next. Things are about to get very serious."

Cozzig shifts into ball form and starts bouncing up and down.

"But if things start to get **too** serious, I'll be there to shut that down right away."

He bounces up and then lands on the table right in front of Cynthia.

"I'll bounce that seriousness right out the door!"

He then rolls back and forth across the table.

"What are we waiting for guys? Let's get this ball rolling!"

Cozzig barrels off the table and onto Ledford's lap.

"You guys don't want to just sit around all day, do you?"

Walker lifts Cozzig off of his lap and pushes him back over to Cynthia.

"Can we vote to kick out members?"

Cynthia shrugs as Cozzig changes back to humanoid form.

"Don't worry, I'll shape up. We'll form a nice bond, you and I."

Chapter 39

After school, at the end of the fundraising period, Ace and his friends are gathered in the auditorium with the rest of the fifth grade students to collect their prizes.

"I've been so excited for this moment I couldn't even sleep last night." Ace informs.

"No, you've been so excited for this moment that **I** couldn't even sleep last night." Grant complains. "You were rocking the bed so hard I felt like I was on a raft out on the ocean."

"I'm just so excited for me to be announced as the winner. I can't even stand it!"

Ace grabs Grant by the arm and flings him to the ground.

"Aw yeah!"

"Here comes Miss Brick with the results." Parker declares.

Ace skips over to his teacher and tries to rip the paper out of her hand but she pulls it out of the way before he can.

"Excuse me. You asked me to be the impartial judge for this. If you'd settle down I could read you all the results."

"Whatever. I'd only change the winner if it wasn't me." Ace grumbles.

"Exactly. Now, in fifth place we have Grant with two boxes."

"You suck Grant." Ace taunts his brother right as he gets back to his feet.

"In fourth place we have Parker with ten boxes."

"You suck Parker."

"Hardly. I may have lost this contest to you, Ace, but I'm clearly winning life."

"In third place we have Curtis with two hundred boxes."

"You…"

Curtis quickly places his hand over Ace's mouth.

"Don't even."

"And that means our big winner is...Rash! With a final total of fifty thousand boxes. Ace, you're in second with twenty-five thousand one hundred and two boxes. You boys should get in line to get your prizes. And congratulations to you Rash."

"Hey, Miss Brick., why'd you put Rash ahead of me?" Ace wonders. "Wasn't I supposed to win?"

"He sold almost twice as many boxes as you. Why wouldn't he be placed ahead of you?"

"But how the hell did that happen? **How**?"

"It **is** a secret but since you're my best friend I can tell you." Rash explains. "Once my dad saw all the boxes that you bought and then littered all over our property, he said there was no way that he was going to let you win. He took out two mortgages on our house and a loan from some especially shady characters in order to have enough money to hand you a humiliating defeat. He said it wasn't enough just to win enough anymore, he had to destroy you. It worked. I won."

"Yes, it definitely sounds like you're the winner in all of this." Parker says sarcastically. "Not only is your family now being crushed under the weight of colossal debt, but you are also now burdened with fifty thousand boxes of turkey balls, which are essentially worthless."

"Curtis will take 'em. Won't you Curtis?"

"For free?"

"At a reduced price."

"Then no."

"Okay free." Rash relents.

"Okay I'll take them then. We already leased a huge warehouse for our new business."

"Cool. You guys want to give my fifty bucks now?"

"No." Ace replies.

"But you have to."

"He hasn't even given me the fifty bucks from **our** bet yet." Parker informs.

"I'll pay you both in turkey balls."

"No, you'll pay me in money. Right now." Rash commands.

"But I don't have the money."

"Oh yes you do. One of the prizes is a one hundred dollar bill. You'll have enough money to pay back me and Parker at the same time."

"Not if I run away with it in my A.P.T. first."

"We'll see about that."

Grant, Curtis, and Parker have already gotten their prizes when Rash beats Ace in a race to the line. As Ace gets seated in his A.P.T with his stack of prizes, Rash is already seated in his own A.P.T. and waits for his friend's next move. Ace notices what Rash is planning and slowly wheels his A.P.T. in the direction of the door.

"You'll never catch me alive!"

Ace commands his machine to charge for the exit, only to ram it over the edge of the auditorium stage instead. He and his prizes spill out all over the floor. Rash climbs out of his A.P.T. and down from the stage to stand above his fallen friend.

"Hey, you caught me."

"And alive no less."

Rash reaches down for the hundred dollar bill as Ace tries to put the foam football in his hand instead. Rash slaps it out of the way and takes the money.

"It would've been so much easier if you had just given this to me."

"It would've been even easier if you had just let me win."

"Sorry. You're just going to have to try harder to beat me next time."